"YZ Chin's tender and furious _____ .. . . gaze into a black sky; her characters are defiant enough to find light."

—**CATHERINE LACEY**, author of *The Answers*

"Sharp as an old wound that never heals, these linked stories remind us afresh of what it takes to survive in a brutal, racially fraught society."

—**SHIRLEY GEOK-LIN LIM**, author of
Among the White Moon Faces

"No doubt many readers will describe *Though I Get Home* as news from another world with much to teach us about what may be unfamiliar to us. But the true gift of Chin's collection is the way it reminds us that much of what may initially seem unfamiliar is actually shared. Don't we all want to know who we are and what we are capable of? Don't we all want to matter, to be seen, to be heard? Aren't we all capable of desperate measures to achieve those desires? So by all means read YZ Chin's book to expand your understanding of the world, but don't be surprised when along the way you discover more about yourself than you bargained for."

—**KAREN SHEPARD**, author of *Kiss Me Someone*

"A haunting, surprising, and rebellious collection that contains multitudes."

—*KIRKUS REVIEWS* **(starred review)**

"Poignant, like an arrow piercing one's heart."

—**LOUISE MERIWETHER**, author of
Daddy Was a Number Runner

"A welcome read in American contemporary literature and an intimate, complex look into Malaysian culture and politics."

—ANA CASTILLO, author of *Black Dove*

"*Though I Get Home* offers passage into the lives of those struggling for their freedom in a country many Americans know little about. Poignant and striking, each story in YZ Chin's elegant debut will change you in some small way."

—JENNIFER BAUMGARDNER, author of
Look Both Ways

"YZ Chin's skilled weavings of poetic language and unwavering tenderness render a moving portrait of characters caught up in changing, challenging circumstances, and their cemented wills and steadfast grit become hallmarks in the power of storytelling and the power of movement."

—MELISSA R. SIPIN, editor in chief,
TAYO Literary Magazine

THOUGH I
GET HOME

YZ CHIN

FEMINIST
PRESS
AT THE CITY UNIVERSITY
OF NEW YORK
NEW YORK CITY

Published in 2018 by the Feminist Press
at the City University of New York
The Graduate Center
365 Fifth Avenue, Suite 5406
New York, NY 10016

feministpress.org

First Feminist Press edition 2018

This book was made possible thanks to a grant from New York State Council on the Arts with the support of Governor Andrew M. Cuomo and the New York State Legislature.

Grateful acknowledgment is made to the following publications in which various forms of this book's pieces first appeared: *Cha: An Asian Literary Journal, Drunken Boat, Failbetter,* Inpatient Press, *Mascara Literary Review, Northwestern* magazine, *Paper Darts,* and *Solstice Literary Magazine.*

First printing April 2018

Cover and text design by Suki Boynton

Library of Congress Cataloging-in-Publication Data
Names: Chin, YZ, author.
Title: Though I get home / YZ Chin.
Description: First Feminist Press edition. | New York, NY : Feminist Press at the City University of New York, 2018.
Identifiers: LCCN 2017056598 (print) | LCCN 2018000178 (ebook) | ISBN 9781936932177 (ebook) | ISBN 9781936932160 (trade pbk.)
Subjects: LCSH: Young women--Fiction. | Political prisoners--Fiction. | Kamunting (Concentration camp)--Fiction. | Malaysia--Fiction.
Classification: LCC PS3603.H5675 (ebook) | LCC PS3603.H5675 A6 2018 (print) | DDC 813/.6--dc23
LC record available at https://lccn.loc.gov/2017056598

CONTENTS

STRIKE

Hunger pinned her to the bunk. Starvation impaled her through the stomach, keeping her down on the thin mattress, resisting the momentum of her feebly raised head. Her neck strained to bring her vision to the requisite level such that she could observe the movement of sun against her prison walls. The sun was her way of telling time and estimating the next delivery of food.

Not that it mattered now. It was the third week into her detention without trial. She did feel secure, as if nothing would ever happen to her again, until death. The days lost their shape, shedding the definition of hours and minutes. Her body, too, lost its shape, pooling downward, lowering her center of gravity, rooting her toward dirt and dust.

They said she was staging a hunger strike. Isa, on her part, felt that the refusal of food was really to make life behind bars more interesting. The meals they brought to her cell were markers of time, and she had looked forward to the packets of rice and gravy as daily celebrations. But then she'd started feeling like a Pavlovian dog. The nods of the men who handed her sustenance became sinister, laced with degradation. She resented the regular reminders of her weakness and dependency.

After minutes of work, she managed to prop herself up

on one elbow. A rolling wave of dizziness lurched her, listing, tipping. She smiled widely. In her teenage years, when she'd lived a sheltered life, she had tried many times, each attempt lasting days or weeks or months, to go on a diet. It didn't much matter what kind of diets they were, or how much science was behind them. The hope was what she needed. She wished, on the other side of each experiment, to find a slim, beautiful her, standing still with folded hands, waiting.

And now, locked away, she would finally obtain the thinnest body of her life. She dreamed, still smiling, of her wafer physique gliding effortlessly among obstacles thrown up by invisible enemies. Anything anybody erected against her she slipped past with a slight sideways turn of her frame, her arms extended ramrod above her head, as if surrendering, but really evading, winning.

She came to. And was disappointed to feel that she was again flat on her back, her previous progress negated. Shadows swam before her eyes. She opened them. Men. Men were leaning over her, explaining something, but not to her. To each other, or maybe to an unseen observer. She sighed. Rank air filled her nose. Rolling her eyes upward, she caught the glance of one man, who started talking faster.

Hands pressed down on her shoulders, pinning them. A hand touched her lips. Isa suddenly wondered what clothes she was wearing. Whether she wore any.

Another pair of hands caught hold of her ankles. Her mind, wandering, entertained the absurd vision of a single many-limbed being. It had paused its speech when it extended hands and fists to restrain her, but now it started up again. Isa thought it might be expecting a response from her, but she could not understand it. When she opened her mouth to tell it so, fingers slipped through and stretched her lips. She gagged and mush rushed in, filling her.

Of course she tried to spit. Of course she thrashed. At first. Then the mush began to acquire flavor and become more than texture. It tasted first like somebody else's vomit, and then like her own. And then it became her, and she was being force-fed herself.

She reclosed her eyes. Up floated a piece of advice from her dead father, given a lifetime ago. What to do when overpowered by a criminal, such as a robber or a rapist: Do not fight. Survival should be your only focus. Everything other than your continued breathing—be it jewelry, money, body, honor—is expendable. Save your life. Do not fight.

Oatmeal. That was what they were forcing into her mouth.

THE BUTLER
OPENS THE DOOR

"All of us had English accents," Grandfather said in an English accent. *Ooloovus.* "That was how we learned, you know. From the British." Grandfather was known to have been employed by the colonizers as a butler, the only one anyone had ever heard of in the middling town of Butterworth, Malaya. But he wasn't a butler. His employer had called him that both because Grandfather's real name was hard to remember and because the British gentleman was forever exasperated by Grandfather's inability to perform everything just as he wished.

"But there is no ice, sir. That is why lemonade is lukewarm."

"But I was helping in kitchen, sir. I did not hear you call."

"But I did not know what corned beef hash is, sir. I thought maybe there would be actual corn."

The gentleman, pushed to his limits, stood up sternly and placed his palms flat against the dinner table. "But! But! But! That is always your excuse! Quite a perverse tropical *but*ler you are!"

And that is how Grandfather became known as a butler. His chief job was to soothe the trauma of World War II inflicted upon his employer. The Japanese had fled after their emperor's surrender, and the British had moved back in on their heels, much like how years later Grandfather would stage a triumphant return to his house after fleeing a pest infestation, waving off rat-poison fumes with both hands. He had saved up ever so many years to afford it, but when the British trudged back into town in 1945, he had nary a thought about ever becoming a homeowner.

In postwar Malaya, the British decided they did not like what the previous tenants had done. Many buildings were reclaimed, repainted, and renamed, including the "rest house" Grandfather knocked on for a job. Just a week prior, the single-story house had been a makeshift Japanese army headquarters. There had been uniformed people always rushing in and out of the place, and Grandfather had known enough to stay far away.

Now the soldiers were gone, and out had come rattan lounge chairs arranged haphazardly in the tiny garden fronting the house, wherever shade could be obtained. White men sagged the chairs with eyes closed and legs akimbo. Working around them, a Malay man replaced weeds with flora that would not survive the weather. A different brown man painted the outside walls with stripes of red, white, and blue. A plaque went up that said "Britannia."

Grandfather would tell me these stories about his past whenever Mama went to dye her hair at the salon, which was once a week. When he first told me he worked at a rest house, I felt shock and shame because the image conjured in my mind was of my grandfather cleaning our conquerors' toilets, his sleeves and cuffs rolled up. But Grandfather roared with his peculiar laugh and told me that nobody ever said "restroom" until after I was born, and anyway a "rest house" was a fancy place for big-shot

British officials to eat, drink, and nap. Sometimes a missionary or two would visit too.

Grandfather had no inkling of what work British men might want done, but he saw the Malay men painting walls and gardening and thought he could do those things just as well as they could. So he borrowed a shirt and went to the rest house.

At his destination, he paused with the tips of his shoes barely touching the cultivated grass, slyly scrutinizing the snoozing men on the lawn. They did not look like they would enjoy interruptions. Grandfather lifted one hand to shield his eyes from the sun. The rest house's door was ajar, but he could not see more than a few feet beyond the threshold. The veranda blocked light, halted it from entry.

He looked back at the garden, where the Malay gardener crouched as if preparing to pray, big fat sweat beads on his forehead. Grandfather envied him. It sure beat being a tin-mine coolie. That stint had left his hands raw, nearly skinless, and he had heard men who worked there for too long died coughing blood. People said they hacked so hard their lungs exploded, and that's why blood came up.

He strode quickly through the doorway, hoping he would run into a white man as near the entrance as possible. It would not do to be taken for a thief in an empty British fancy house.

There was no one in the first room he found. He scratched just above his belly button. He was not used to wearing a shirt. It sure was cool in there, almost breezy. He looked up and there was a vortex above sending down supernatural winds. He had heard of ceiling fans, but had never before stood under one.

Someone coughed behind him. Grandfather jumped. It was a white man with a mustache and hair that looked like a hat.

"Saa," Grandfather said quickly. He put his hand over his heart. He had seen this gesture, he could not remember where, and he knew it denoted respect.

And that was how Grandfather got hired at the rest house. The white man he met, Mr. Burgess, had been doubtful at first. He was a new arrival to Malaya, and it had been explained to him that, for administrative tasks, Macaulay's children were best on account of their pliant character, while for manual labor a Malay would do, but they were by nature lazy and needed supervision, which explained the white men keeping watch on the lawn out front. As for Chinks, they were mendacious drug users and should not be trusted.

In the end, Grandfather was allowed to stay because Mr. Burgess had a teenage daughter who was afraid of the Indians and the Malays working in the house. The tender flower, poor thing, would tremble whenever one of them walked past. They scrupulously avoided eye contact, but it wasn't their gaze that terrified her so. It was because they were so swarthy. Grandfather, with his skin somewhere between yellow and orange, was very much less traumatic for young Miss Lily. Miss Lily had hazel eyes and long wavy hair the color of straw. To Grandfather she was as exotic as a ceiling fan.

Mama didn't like Grandfather telling me his stories. She said they would give me nightmares. I didn't see how. Back then, the things that gave me nightmares came out of *Teletubbies*, this new program on TV. Mama was adamant though. It was a good thing she needed to dye her hair so

8

often, even though she was not even forty and people often flattered her by asking if we were siblings.

Grandfather became the only person allowed to serve Miss Lily whenever she visited the rest house. Mr. Burgess spent an inordinate amount of time there, reading and ordering dishes no one knew how to make, like pork chops and pudding. Miss Lily, on the other hand, was not difficult to serve. Most of the time she simply wanted some attention. It was easy enough for Grandfather to smile and say "Good, good" whenever she ran to show him interesting weeds cradled in her palms, even if he was slightly repulsed by her at first.

By the time Grandfather had more or less mastered English, he knew that there was no Mrs. Burgess. There had been one, but she did not cross the ocean with her husband and daughter, whether dead or dead set against moving to the colonies Grandfather was never told.

Mama would get livid whenever she found Grandfather out. "What are you doing to her!" she would shout, pointing to me without looking at me, which made me feel stupid. Once, she mentioned a name that sounded British, exciting my curiosity. Were there stories about other British people Grandfather had been holding back from me?

Grandfather's face had borne a look of amazed anger when she said the name. And then he had looked confused.

The better Grandfather understood English, the more unreasonable Mr. Burgess's requests became, to the point that after a few years, Grandfather would sometimes pretend not to understand what the gentleman was saying. If Mr. Burgess showed signs of inebriety, but drawled at Grandfather to bring him more port, Grandfather would emerge ten minutes later with a steaming dish of Chinese food.

"But I thought you wanted 'pork,' sir. This is pork, you asked for it, very good, taste good."

Or he would invent an excuse to bring Miss Lily into the room, slyly encouraging Mr. Burgess to put on his best behavior.

In time Miss Lily got over her fear of the natives, but Grandfather remained her favorite. She became fascinated with the dialect Grandfather spoke, and often asked him to tell her stories about the land he had left in search of a better life. She asked him again and again to describe the poverty and the lack of hope, nodding in sympathy when he concluded, each time, with a resigned sigh, that he'd had no choice but to leave home and come to Malaya.

She said her own father would never tell her why they had left England. He always put her off, saying that one day, when the time was right and she was old enough to understand, he would. But she felt quite old enough—did the British ladies not frequently compliment her on her beauty? What a graceful, pretty thing, they would exclaim. And indeed, she cut a fine figure, standing as tall as Grandfather when she remembered to keep her carriage erect. The tropics had given her cheeks a roseate glow, and her demeanor was open and friendly because she had never yet met a person unkind to her in her life.

Mama cried so hard at Grandfather's funeral that she could not speak. When I touched her and tried to comfort her, she grabbed and squeezed me with her arms, her two hands covering my ears on each side, pressing down hard. She muffled the world. I was baffled by the gesture. It felt simultaneously like protection, and also like robbery.

o

As Miss Lily blossomed, Grandfather transitioned from being almost a nanny to being a bodyguard of sorts for her. He wasn't quite a chaperone, but he could facilitate the increased independence expected for a young woman from a good family by conveying her to recreation clubs, music lessons, tea parties, and the like. He purchased trinkets to which she took a fancy at local stores, so that she never had to worry about carrying her own money.

Meanwhile, Mr. Burgess was giving serious thought to the advice he had received regarding his daughter's future. After all, she was already one score and one. She would fare a better marriage in London society, and although the education she had received from her English tutors here was not lacking, Lily Burgess would still benefit from mixing with more young people of her own kind. He had listened at the club, drink in hand, to all the well-meaning matrons who took pity on the motherless girl. And he was well set on heeding their counsel when Lily disappeared.

By this point it had been five years into his move to the colonies, and Mr. Burgess had thought all possibility of danger long past. He had been uncommonly paranoid and suspicious of calamity the first year, watchful over his property and his daughter, but to have danger strike now, when he felt almost at ease, almost sure of himself in this strange land! Even his body had adjusted to the climate, no longer sweating torrents at the slightest contact with the outdoors. It felt like an ambush of the blackest kind.

A search party was quickly organized, every white man in the area having volunteered. All work stalled; nobody, British or otherwise, could focus enough to do anything. It was like the days when airplanes flew noisily overhead, dropping propaganda, when speculations literally floated in the air and everybody clamored to make predictions, trying to outsmart what would become history.

Where could she have gone? Everyone's worst fear was that she had run off with a native beau, heaven forfend. But nothing could be gained from questioning all the gardeners and cooks and shoe shiners and such. Suppose she had gotten wind of her father's plan to move them back to England and had felt somehow reluctant to leave, having formed an attachment to her residence of the past few years? But what fashionable young girl would forfeit the interesting bustle of London for a tropical outpost?

They searched the nearby hills and their waterfalls, their brooks and streams. They parted foliage and whacked their way through wild bushes. Grandfather led them into parts of town where no white man went, translating for them the replies of bewildered men, women, and children in oversized rags. Except most of the time they needed no translation, their heads emphatically shaking, smelling trouble.

It took just one day and one night to break Mr. Burgess. He was yet reasonably contained when the search party agreed by consensus to suspend its efforts, due to the darkness of nightfall. But the father went wild when morning came and Miss Lily did not turn up. He accused anyone he saw of abducting his daughter. Grandfather got the worst of it because he stoically insisted on serving Mr. Burgess his meals and fetching him his papers just as before. When Mr. Burgess hurled all kinds of insults—calling him a scoundrel, a blackguard, a ruffian—Grandfather simply averted his eyes and coaxed his employer to eat in a monotonous voice void of emotion. For once, he had no "buts" to offer.

Grandfather persisted. He thought having his usual

routine would help moor Mr. Burgess. When that didn't work, Grandfather did what he could to introduce distraction, risking insolence to ask for recipes of classic English dishes from the flow of visitors now coming every hour to see the man placed under such painful trials.

"But it will make Mr. Burgess forget," he would say. He never said "happy"; it was always "forget."

"Be strong and put your faith in God," the visitors advised Mr. Burgess, the ladies making sure to be standing at least three feet away on account of his aura of intoxication.

Time passed, and the visitors stopped coming. She must have left town, perhaps even the colony, they said. Sometimes young people lose their heads, a few commented. On the other hand, there were hushed whispers about white slavery, a horrible fate. Were there not still living sultans in this barbaric land, even if they had been stripped of power and had to pay tribute to the British? Mrs. Windshuttle's cousin's secretary swore on a true story, about a girl just like Lily, who was now in chains and feeding grapes to an obese old chieftain of some sort in Borneo, across the waters.

Grandfather made sure none of this gossip reached Mr. Burgess. He thought it a good thing that Mr. Burgess's people had stopped coming around, prying and disturbing the peace. He had acted as a shield as best he could, but anyone could see Mr. Burgess had no fight left. He drank at all hours of the day and did nothing except scour newspapers and local pamphlets for signs of his girl. When he got into one of his dark moods, he abused Grandfather until he tired himself out. Grandfather bore it all.

"But sir is drinking too much," he would venture. Sometimes he even wrestled bottles away, holding them in custody and promising Mr. Burgess, "But if you eat as much as you drink, you can drink as much as you want."

○

Once, I asked my parents why I had no brothers or sisters. I was feeling lonely, with no one to admire the Lego castles I painstakingly built, or to be jealous of my newly acquired rollerblading skills. At my question, Father and Mama fixed their eyes on their plates, their mouths making chewing motions. They ignored me.

Everyone knew Miss Lily was dead when the rest house became haunted a year later. Spoons flew across rooms and headless geckos turned up in all corners of the place. An insistent, regular thumping could be heard in the afternoons, the sounds of someone methodically clomping up stairs, except the rest house was single story and had no stairs to speak of.

The fact that Miss Lily had become a ghost surprisingly gained ground without resistance among all communities, from hired labor to enlightened colonizers. It spanned cultures and beliefs and experiences and intellects. The visitors once more took interest in That Poor Man, including new arrivals who had not been around for the previous year's heartrending drama.

Mr. Burgess was by now greatly changed. He had ceased to leave the rest house months ago. He looked as sallow and sleepy as a lotus eater, except the lotus he ate was full of bitter sorrow. He alone had to be taught that the supernatural events around him were proof that his daughter was no more. Because of his dilapidated state, everyone assumed that he had long ago accepted his loss, and therefore the news could not add so very much to his pain, but they learned their mistake when Mr. Burgess shot himself in the chest with a pistol.

Luckily the wound was not mortal. Naturally, it fell upon Grandfather to treat Mr. Burgess's injuries and to nurse him back to health. Even the white doctor summoned from the next, bigger town conceded that Grandfather was doing Mr. Burgess good. "Keep changing those rags," he gruffly instructed, though he could see with his own eyes that that was precisely what Grandfather had been doing on his own initiative.

Grandfather liked to say that this was when he had acquired his stooped back, from constantly bending over a prone, moaning Mr. Burgess. I would get piggyback rides on Father's shoulders, sometimes even Mama's, but Grandfather never gave me any rides, and I had been told that it was because he had a bad back.

"But I can do it," I remembered Grandfather saying.

My parents never relented.

Grandfather latched on to the idea of a funeral to motivate Mr. Burgess. As ideas went it was a strange one, but Grandfather could think of no better. In his mind, if Mr. Burgess could not be induced to get well and leave his bed for his own precious daughter's funeral, nothing would do the trick. And so Grandfather set to work making preparations, airing out what he judged Miss Lily's prettiest dresses, and searching through Mr. Burgess's trunks for a photograph.

But Mr. Burgess could not be moved. He groaned and tried to shift positions in bed, which simply set off more waves of pain—perhaps that was what he wanted, to feel pain.

"Do as you wish," he finally growled, his teeth clenched and bared.

Grandfather shook his head. "But funeral is for Miss Lily," he said.

Mr. Burgess managed to turn himself over and lay facing the wall, panting.

So it came to pass that Miss Lily's last rites caused a great commotion and upheaval among the town's residents. The British community was aghast at the handwritten "invitations" that turned up on their doorsteps, informing them in almost but not quite impeccable English that a wake would be held at the rest house— at the rest house! The note also begged their pardon and asked them to "please excuse the different pastor." It was plain that the messages had been written by Mr. Burgess's butler, and the thought that Mr. Burgess had slipped so far brought a fresh wave of visitors to his sick bed. To no avail did they try to dissuade him from entrusting everything to his butler, who was, after all, not of their kind. A few men and women even volunteered themselves, deigning to overstep the boundaries of convention for the sake of not having Mr. Burgess humiliate himself further. But he turned them all down.

Nothing yet prepared them, those who dressed up for the wake out of curiosity or some last shred of pity and respect, for the shocking spectacle awaiting them at the rest house. For it was not at all the proper Christian rites due to an innocent girl taken in her prime by the Lord, who caused everything to happen for a reason. What greeted them was instead some kind of barbaric ritual, the rest house suffused with incense smoke and the toxic smell of things burning. Besides Grandfather, who was doing things the only way he knew how, there was a heretic dressed in yellow robes fussing with his silly hat in the corner. Wait—was he—was he putting on makeup?

Preposterous! Some of the guests turned on their heels and left immediately. Even sympathy had its limits, and

God helped only those who helped themselves. Mr. Burgess was obviously a lost cause.

Bowing at everyone who walked in, Grandfather ignored the glares and mutterings directed at him, busying himself instead with various small tasks, something which was, after all, his job. He straightened and restraightened the huge framed black-and-white image of Miss Lily near the entrance, the first thing anyone would see when they entered, providing their eyes had adjusted to the clouds of noxious smoke. Miss Lily was not smiling in this picture. Her expression was mock serious, as if obeying a camera-man who had asked her to look dignified.

"It smells like an opium den in here," whispered a woman to her husband, glancing meaningfully at Grandfather. "I dare say," murmured the husband in response.

About half a dozen stayed on because, at the end of the day, they could not entirely abandon Mr. Burgess; astray though he was, he was *one of them*. And of course, there was the morbid need to see for themselves what would happen. At least they outnumbered the heretics who had hijacked the wake—perhaps they could even override the two? They could quickly nip back for a Bible, or dispatch someone . . .

But no such luck, for here came an entire village more of barbarians, bent on ferrying away the poor girl's soul. A few of them were recognizable as rickshaw drivers or washer-women whose services had previously been contracted, but for the most part the throng looked strange and yet oddly familiar, by dint of their resemblance to one another. They stuck fresh joss sticks in the incense pot, crowding it until it looked like an overused horizontal archery target.

A coffin stretched out behind Miss Lily's framed face. Someone had hung a garland of white and yellow flowers over the photograph, forming a second frame. Grandfather beckoned at the guests to come forward. But there were so many bodies squeezed into the space. The white people felt it would not do for them to rub shoulders with the newcomers, whom they gathered were hired mourners paid to stand in as Miss Lily's family and friends. Disgraceful!

Eventually, some kind of system was forged out of the chaos. The British watched in amazement as the disingenuous actors formed a single-file line and walked one by one around the coffin, counterclockwise. They each paused at the head of the box and peered down, presumably at an opening where Miss Lily's beautiful face would be. But there was no body, was there? They had never found her.

From a muted commotion among the hired mourners the British guests hazarded that the savages were—believe it or not—also shocked by the unconventionality of the wake. Indignant, the British traded hypotheses among themselves, growing pink with exertion. What, were made-up prayers and false gods too good for a white woman? They should know it was the other way around!

Then they, too, wended their way toward the coffin. Here the incense haze grew thicker. Someone sneezed. "God—!" said a Mrs. Maycock. She had meant to say "God bless you," but once the first word was out she realized that she had not seen the sneezer, who could very well have been one of the heretics.

"Lord have mercy!" The first white person to reach the head of the coffin stiffened back in horror. Mrs. Maycock, disregarding the measured shuffling of the counterclockwise procession, pushed forward, looked down, and gasped.

The coffin indeed had a viewing panel of sorts at the head, offering a neck-up look at the deceased. Except instead of a serene face, Mrs. Maycock was staring, upside down, at a different picture of Miss Lily, this time smiling broadly, and she would have looked like an angel had someone not colored her stretched lips with a garish red, an amateur hand that barely stayed inside the lines. This picture was unframed, and at its bottom it was joined with the collar of a frilly white dress, smoothed out and laid flat.

"You!" Mrs. Maycock said, whirling around and almost pointing a finger at Grandfather.

He winced. "Makeup is tradition," he explained apologetically. He knew his hand had been shaking. He was sorry; he felt sorry for everyone.

Mrs. Maycock wanted to pick it up with him further, but the decked-out heretic in the corner advanced forward with a dinging handbell, waving her and everyone else away from the coffin by flapping his robes.

There was a long, ominous pause as he made his eyes big and surveyed the crowd, seemingly looking into everyone's eyes in turn. Then, without warning, stentorian streams of chants emerged from him, accompanied by spasmodic handbell rings. It must have sounded like a strange tongue to the outsiders, its long plains of steady tones suddenly giving way to peaks of plaintive cries. The hired mourners got to work almost immediately, echoing parts of the voodoo sounds at intervals. A few of them had a different task, that of wailing insensibly and performing grief.

Nobody left, even though it was a truly eerie scene. After about twenty minutes of chanting and ringing the mercenary mourners all got up and stood side by side in a line facing the coffin. At a gesture from the costumed man they all bowed to their waist as one. Whenever they bent their bodies, their heads and shoulders and backs gave way to Miss Lily's unsmiling visage, revealing it to the spectators at the back of the room, only to obscure it again when they straightened. Reveal, obscure. Reveal, obscure. Three times they repeated this part of the ritual, and then, finally, quiet. One after another, the hired mourners now silently lit stacks of paper on fire and dropped them into a wide but shallow metal basin.

"It looks like counterfeit money," someone said in a hushed, awed voice.

Then came papier-mâché houses, cars, horses, even a pair of people, man and woman. The British guests gazed in heightened amazement as these, too, were set on fire in turn. "She must have loved the arts and crafts, bless her soul," they said.

Fed by those offerings, the fire blazed, shaking loose thick gray smoke that undulated upward to intertwine with clouds of incense. Soon, it formed a screen separating the living from the coffin.

Quite a show, some of the visitors would later say, as casually as they could. It was the talk of the town for months.

Grandfather told me this story four times, always when Mama was out dyeing her hair. I liked this story because Grandfather would slip into a kind of trance, delivering the narrative as if it had happened to someone else, or as if he were a stranger talking about Grandfather's life. I could never tell if he was proud of what he had done. All but one time he went into a reverie after finishing the tale, staring fixedly at his creased palms, his head bowed by his hunched back. The time that was different, he ended the story by saying that the haunting had stopped sixteen years ago, and that I could go see for myself at the rest house, still standing in the center of town. Then he gave me a long look and asked if I wanted some ice cream.

Once, at the dinner table, I asked about my grandmother, who had died long before I was born. Was she pretty? A silence expanded like a smoke bomb. After a while, Grandfather smiled weakly at me. He leaned over and pinched my chin. And then he stared for a long time into my eyes, his irises two hard kernels. He looked like he wanted to say something important, but perhaps it was nothing more than another one of his entertaining stories. When his mouth finally moved, Mama made a loud sound, something between a cough and a grunt. Grandfather let go of my chin. I supposed he thought I was asking because I was insecure about my looks, especially my eyes. They are not like other people's eyes, which are black and uncomplicated. My irises have two or three colors, depending on the position of the sun. They contain shades of brown, and sometimes they become like glass, fragile and watery. I hated them. I didn't want to be different, a freak.

And now Grandfather has been gone for two years, and Mama more silent than ever. She no longer bothers dyeing her hair, which is naturally tainted with odd streaks of rust, as if her hair were just like real metal and required regular polishing.

I miss Grandfather. I often think about his stories—how intoxicating they were because they were forbidden, made taboo by Mama. But now that I am an adult I can do whatever I want. I told her I am going to England in a week, a trip made possible by my inheritance from Grandfather. She did not ask me the reason for my visit. But she did ask, "How far must you go?"

"London is more than six thousand miles away," I said.

A BET IS PLACED

Across the street is a KFC. I see a lot of young people with motorbike helmets tucked under their arms go in there, pushing the glass doors inward and letting out a blast of air-conditioned air. I'm an old man now, so they say, but I still like to pay attention to what young people do, so that I can communicate with my grandchildren. My grandkids sure do like their KFC, although none of them are old enough to ride motorbikes yet. I'm not sure if I want to live long enough to hear about their first road accidents, actually. I know everyone has those; it's part of growing up. But the way I see these youngsters weave in and out of traffic on their bikes, it worries me.

I pride myself on being much more open-minded than other men my age, really. The KFC, for one. I eat there sometimes, with my youngest daughter and her husband and child when they visit me. I can't cook so much anymore, not like I used to. Tossing meat and vegetables in a wok the right way strains your wrist a lot. Besides, my daughter decided for me years ago that I hate cooking. She tells her daughter the story of how I used to be a cook at the rest house, where all the British civil servants liked to congregate and relax after work. She emphasizes how I could make pork chops and scones and all that English stuff, but could not pronounce the names of the dishes "properly" because I was born in mainland China. She stresses this fact as if it were very important.

My daughter also uses that story to explain why she never cooks. She talks of how I always made her help out in the English kitchen, how terrible that was. Her story always ends with how happy she was when Merdeka was declared and the British left. I never knew she was that happy. She did not show it. Just a girl of five.

Anyways. I am a modern-minded old man, not like other men my age. For example, Ah Kao sitting across the table from me here. He has one leg up on the edge of his chair, twitching to some beat only he can hear. His once-white singlet is pulled up to rest just under his nipples, exposing his Tiger beer belly to the scant breeze. "It's too hot," he always complains. Whenever I tell him to stop exposing his crotch and put his leg down, he cackles and says, "At least I'm not wearing a sarong!"

Ah Kao has a good heart though. He's just stubborn and set in his ways. His children and grandchildren don't love him as much as mine do me. Another favorite topic of his is how his kin never visit him. I always tell him to try some KFC, just across the street from where we sit every day, but he always goes "Ahhhhhhh!" in an irritated tone and spits on the ground. He says air-conditioning makes his skin itch. I say it's because he doesn't shower, and the others laugh. Our jokes repeat a lot, but I like it that way. There's Ah Kao and me and Lao Ping and Mr. Yap. Sometimes Vasan takes a break from his roti canai stall and joins us.

"So, five ringgit today?" Lao Ping, ever eager, puts his hand in his pocket and asks. "I call five minutes past three!"

I look at the sky, thinking. It's blue enough, but you can

just see a tinge of black clouds in the direction of Ipoh, capital of the best chicken rice in Malaysia. This is why I like sitting here with my friends. I can see the sky unobstructed because there are no walls and no doors blocking my view, and Lao Ping's cigarette smoke is carried away by the wind soon enough. I'm sure my grandchildren think roadside stalls are out of fashion, but if I am willing to eat at KFC, I'm sure they can tolerate the idea of me sitting in a big shed with an atap roof and wooden beams.

I look at the sky again. Then I crane my neck to look at the old clock hanging from a nail pounded into one of the wooden beams. That's our official clock. Last year we had Mr. Yap's son-in-law climb on top of two benches stacked together, with us holding the legs steady, so that he could hammer that nail in and hang the clock up. It was all because Ah Kao had cheated one day. Now we have an official clock that's too high up for any of us to tamper with, and fair's fair.

The clock says half past noon. I think about it a bit more, then take five ringgit out of my wallet. "Seven minutes before three." Lao Ping gives me a look. I match it. Mr. Yap laughs. Lao Ping asks him if he's putting money down or what.

We flag Vasan down the next time he's passing by our table to bring his customers their plates of roti canai. "Betting again today?" he asks. "Sure we are," we chorus. He laughs, nods, and goes on his way. We can always count on him to be a fair judge, that Vasan.

It's not even one o'clock. We have hours. Ah Kao had called half past three and Mr. Yap had said none today, a bold move on his part. So we sit on our benches, Ah Kao with his belly exposed again. My grandchildren always ask how I can sit for so long on those benches without backs.

Doesn't my spine hurt? I tell them that's how I've always sat. My youngest daughter tells them to leave me be. She tells them how lucky they are that they don't have to stay on their feet all day in a hot, stuffy kitchen, making food for ghost people. I don't want to be the kind of old man who says things like that, but I can't stop her disciplining her own child, or even her nieces and nephews, can I?

In our roadside stall we wait for the occasional breeze to shift our positions. Now and then we look at the sky. We have hours to go. The smell of fried oysters from the stall behind me jostles with the smell of grease from KFC. I like my spot, right here on this particular bench, because I can always choose which smell to take in. If I concentrate on fried oysters, the KFC smell goes away, and vice versa. I like that.

A strong breeze blows. The rain tree right next to our table shudders and sheds a few leaves onto our table. One leaf falls into my Milo kosong. I pick it out and let it drop its wet weight to the ground. This is what we get for moving our table so close to the edge of the curb, but Ah Kao always complains that it's hot, so we do it every day unless it's already raining by the time we arrive.

Almost half past two. We start paying more attention now, perusing the clouds, checking the visibility of Maxwell Hill on the horizon. Mr. Yap plucks a leaf off the rain tree next to us and rubs his finger back and forth across its surface. He always says it's his secret method, and I always say, "Just look at your track record; it obviously doesn't work." The others always laugh. We like our old jokes.

The glass doors of KFC open. The breeze has died down, so my bare thigh feels a slight hint of the air-conditioning. Two white people come out, a man and a woman. I wonder why they're here. The last white tourist I saw was years ago. It was a man alone with his very big backpack. See, there's nothing to do here in Taiping. These two, they look like they are in their forties. They do not have yellow hair. One of the most common misconceptions of white people is that they all have yellow hair, while the truth is that most of them have brown hair. I know this because I used to work in the rest house.

The white people stand outside the glass doors for a while, talking and blocking the way when a few other people try to get out of KFC. They apologize and move to the side. Suddenly the woman looks up and catches my eye. I shift my glance away quickly. When I next try to sneak a look at them, they are walking across the street, headed straight for our table. Mr. Yap and Lao Ping are arguing about something. They don't notice. But I see that Ah Kao, too, is looking at them warily. I wish he would pull his singlet down.

"Excuse me." The man stops a few feet away from our table. Having no walls can be a bad thing after all, I think to myself.

The man tries again. "Excuse me, could I ask you gentlemen a question?" My brain will not work, even though I have heard "excuse me" plenty of times before.

"HALLO!" Ah Kao says. What is it about people raising their voices when they don't know what they're saying? I wish he would at least put his leg down.

"Hi there. Hello." The man looks a little taken aback. "I was wondering if you knew the way to the jail?"

Lao Ping starts sniggering. He leans over and gives me a shove, speaking in Hokkien: "Eh, he's talking to you!"

"He's talking to all of us," I point out.

"You're the one who used to work for the ghost people, right?" He sniggers some more.

I look at Lao Ping's face, and I don't like what I see, so I turn to the man and say, "I know."

"Great!" The man looks relieved. "How do we get there?"

I hesitate. The words come slow, but they come, and soon they are coming faster. "I know how you can get to jail, but why do you want to go there?"

The woman chuckles a little. The man turns to her and smiles briefly before talking to me. "We've heard that it's the oldest jail in Malaysia. Is that true?"

I tell them yes, and I tell them that we also have the oldest railway station, the oldest museum, and the oldest zoo. I tell them everything used to happen here in Taiping. They have a little difficulty understanding me, but they nod a lot to make up for it. I tell them how to get to the jail. And then I tell them to buy an umbrella because it's going to rain seven minutes before three. They laugh as if it were a joke, not a bettor's instinct honed by years of sitting right here.

Ah Kao is jealous. I can see it. "What did you tell them?" he asks as soon as they start walking away.

I look at the clock. It's almost ten minutes to three. "I told them it's going to rain soon," I say, looking squarely into Ah Kao's eyes. Mr. Yap laughs, and Lao Ping jokingly calls me a race traitor.

"You'll see," I smile and say. I am confident that I will win the bet today. The rain will fall at exactly seven minutes to three. I will laugh and scoop up the money in the middle of the table. Ah Kao will try to guilt me into buying him a cup of teh tarik before we leave, and on my way home, I will get my favorite grandchild fried chicken.

THOUGH SHE
GETS HOME

Isabella Sin turned away from the man preparing her char kuey teow to look up at the sky. It was yet another hot tropical day, and she would rather not watch the beads of sweat on the noodle hawker's face coalesce into a globe that would then start rolling down the slope of his cheek, gathering momentum until, with the man's next energetic slide and toss of his wok, it launches into air, missing the dirty rag draped around his neck to land on her lunch-in-progress without so much as a plip.

The sky blazed blue. Little puffs of white clouds scattered about, their edges jagged, carelessly torn and discarded. Isa narrowed her eyes to locate the sun, just to see where it was. She looked away quickly the moment her vision blurred with brightness. Four and a half miles away, Maxwell Hill roosted on the horizon, and above it hovered dark swathes of monsoon clouds, nothing like the trifles hanging over her head. It would rain later today, no doubt.

Isa caught herself and shook her head, half smiling. According to family legend, both her grandfathers had been competent cooks, but here she was, waiting her turn for greasy street food. Her cooking was so terrible that no one wanted to marry her—that was Isa's mother's pet theory number one. Pet theory number two blamed Isa's marital status on her beige-flecked eyes and propensity to speak proper English. These traits were simply too off-putting to local men, who thought her stuck up beyond words. "Too good for Manglish, izzit?" some would sneer. "If you like speaking like ang moh why you stay here lah?" others puzzled. Like the town of Taiping itself, she was too globalized to attract those seeking unalloyed rural peace and quiet, and yet not sophisticated enough to be metropolitan chic. A year in London had ruined her, Isa's mother said. She should never have gone. And all she had to show for it was family shame coursing through her veins, her grandparents' illicit marriage sheening her irises pale topaz under strong sunlight.

Among her inheritance was the highly practical gift of rain betting. Today's first raindrops would fall around 3:15 p.m. Isa squinted at the hills and nodded. Gong Gong had been a local legend in the field. Even after he'd become chairbound, he insisted on perching in front of the largest, best window of the house. When it did rain, he grinned gap-toothed and victorious at drizzling skies while Isa hurried to jam the jalousie window panes shut, for fear of the old man getting drenched.

At least he was really, really good at something, Isa thought wistfully, entering the shade of her office building. She used to want to be a writer. She'd spent years writing poetry and starting the Great Malaysian Novel. Now here she was, almost thirty, writing ad copy in a town whose biggest advertising opportunities lay in calls to franchise global brands like Starbucks and KFC. She and the town, they were both forever playing catch-up, waiting for trends to play out elsewhere before catching the last carriage of a train pulling away.

At 2:59 p.m. Isa peered out the window closest to her desk. The remains of her lunch lay next to her in a recycling wastebasket meant for paper, wafting smells of refried oil around the air-conditioned space.

Yes, as she'd predicted. The little torn cotton balls from earlier had become black and solid, reminding her of the wads of makeup remover she wiped over her eyes every night. She waved hurried byes to her colleagues and left to collect her clothes hanging out on lines to dry. If she didn't get home before the rain began in earnest, she would have to wash those clothes all over again. She straddled her motorbike and looked up at the skies one last time before kicking the machine to life.

Nobody in town had a dryer. No one that Isa knew, at least. Everyone relied on the sun's wholesome, germ-destroying rays to toast their laundry. Off on the horizon lightning flashed, a heavenly redwood tree spreading golden roots down to earth. Then rain fell. Drat. Her prediction was off after all. She was still a few minutes away from home, but the rain, lazy and steady, had already soaked her back through.

Near the top of a slope, where she could almost see what lay beyond on the other side of the mound, she revved her motorbike. It lurched under her. Together they crested the slope, and then she was pulled into descent. She leaned backward to counter gravity, left hand squeezing, engaging the brakes. The back wheel stiffened and dragged. The motorcycle slid faster anyway. She looked at the houses going by on the left. There was the one with bougainvillea in many colors, next to the mosque. Another where an old man liked to sit on a stone bench abutting his rusty gate. But no one was out now.

Finally, her own gates came into view. Water ran down

her blouse as she dismounted. Next to her the bike hummed, propped up and listing to one side, as she slipped her hand through rusty metal bars to reach for the latch. From the clotheslines strung between two papaya trees, skirts and dress shirts hung heavy, gorged with rain and swaying dully in the wind. She dashed around, pulling them off and cradling their limp carcasses in her arms.

The air smelled faintly of chemicals. Isabella stood at the kitchen sink, rinsing out the tin mug she had used to drain the last of some mystery alcohol she'd found on the top of the fridge. The rain had stopped. Through the kitchen window she could see the washed-out sky, bland like cheap pasar malam clothes after their third wash, all bled out.

Just when she was starting to feel better, it was time to go back to work. She moved her tongue about in her mouth, touching first one cheek, then the other. She had dawdled as long as she could, but the excuse of rain had worn out. From the bedroom she picked through the pile of still-damp clothes for a jacket. It was a short trip to the office, but the winds could be nippy after a bout of rain.

She didn't register the drops of revenant rain until she was on her bike. She cocked her head. The second wave was a pitter patter against her helmet, almost playful, like a wooden fish in the hands of a monk with no sense of tempo. Isa revved the bike. Her neck felt stiff and her tongue was still oddly heavy and clammy from the alcohol. She wanted to course through the drizzle, zipping in and out of slow-moving, cow-like cars. And then rain roared. Without transition, the fickle monsoon weather let loose. Above rooftops, telephone lines thrashed wildly, as if carrying messages so unspeakable they could not bear it. Next door, the antenna on the neighbor's car thrashed about, demonically possessed.

The last scene Isa saw before she rushed into the house was the trees in her compound bending double, clothes-lines yanked taut. She hoped they would not snap in the storm. Overhead, water poured so fast and so hard that it all seemed a vibrating solid block, no individual component discernible. It would be an hour, maybe more, before she could go back to work, and by that time there would be no point. Isa's heart lifted. She thought regretfully of the empty bottle in the garbage.

Still, the afternoon was hers, and the house, hers. She sat down on a rattan chair in the half darkness. The marble floor was chilly against her soles. The house grew dimmer, and soon she could not see very much at all, just dark lumps surrounding her. She thought about getting up to find a book to read—something she hadn't done for a while. But books were no longer about distant worlds and alien people who did unimaginable things. Now she was too old; she knew too much. She couldn't truly inhabit fictional worlds anymore.

She drifted off to the sounds of waterfalls.

The sun was down when Isa woke. Her throat felt parched.

Something was wrong. The house was too dark. It must be raining still. She could hear it, a rushing of water in the background.

She groped her way against furniture and walls to reach the kitchen, flicking on lights as she went. Maybe there was more mystery alcohol to be found, stashed behind fine bowls and trays never brought down to use. Strange, but the more light switches she flipped, the louder the rain sounded, as if her senses were dependent upon each other. And then icy marble turned into lukewarm liquid. Isa yelped. Water eddied about her ankles. All around her, the kitchen was a tank of tepid, dirty broth.

The water invading the house seemed calm, content to mill, but somewhere outside she could hear a different version, angry and unceasing. She stood rigid in her kitchen pool, dazed, looking at the wall clock ticking. She had only been asleep for a little over an hour. How could this have happened?

She saw now that the water, brown with dirt and thick with soil, was coming in fast through the kitchen door sill. That door usually opened to a thin scrap of land on which she grew a pair of hunchback rambutan trees, the favorite toilet of her neighbor's turkeys. She heard the fowl now, cackling like nihilists greeting the end of the world with joy.

Was there a bucket in that cupboard under the sink? The mop was in the hallway closet. And somewhere, gathering dust, was the old-fashioned chamber pot she had accepted, sniggering, from Gong Gong.

The water was creeping up her calves now, translucent nude stockings she was slowly, very slowly, pulling on. Isa felt wild. She wanted to close her hand around the wooden door's knob and swing it wide open to let in the rabble of furious water. It would be better than the maddening slow seep. Toaster, kettle, microwave, tudung saji. Those would be gone soon, ruined by dirt water. Radio, table, chairs, refrigerator? She swept the kitchen, taking inventory.

Thunder sounded directly above. The house dimmed for a beat and the lights flickered twice, as if lightning had been brought indoors, just like the mud and rain. Isa waded out of the kitchen and into the bedroom. Dresser, footrest, gold-embroidered slippers, tacky music box with a lid that did not fully clamp down on overflowing jewelry. She picked the box up, put it down. In the living room, television, jade Buddha statuette, decorative piano no one played. She tried lifting the television, just to see. Too heavy.

Back in the bedroom she found a suitcase that was still half-filled with shirts and underwear, crumpled, and a handkerchief, neatly folded. She shook the clothes out onto the bed, then splashed about filling the suitcase with what she could, trying to be smart about it—was the object's worth equal to the volume of suitcase being taken up? Music box, in. Delicate antique cup, okay. Gong Gong's gold watch, sure.

In no time the suitcase was full. She clamped the lid shut and hoisted it, panting, onto the top of the piano, unsettling a patch of dust. When she clambered back down, the water was waist-high. She would have to leave.

But first, she moved her legs with difficulty and made for the kitchen. In times of emergency, the authorities always advised storing potable water. From above the sink she took down a Sustagen water bottle and started filling it from the purifier hooked up to the faucet. And then she glanced down upon the breadth of water surrounding her, and the absurdity of what she was doing kicked in. She laughed until good water trembled into bad water.

Snorting, she took a half step backward and fell into the bad water. Under the surface, the flood smelled at once rotten and too alive. The urgent gushing above turned into a dull gurgling below, like someone trying to rinse with a chunk of food wedged in one cheek pocket. Isa went into a half-hearted breaststroke. Her feet kept brushing the flood bed. With one last look at the kitchen door (was it bowing?), she paddled her way to the front of the house, fighting the dragging waters. If the scourge was coming in through the back, then perhaps leaving the front door open would allow the house to be more of a conduit and less of a trap, within which the entirety of her things waited, doomed to be ruined.

Her hands slapped the front door. She floated upright. The fear ratcheted up, doubling, tripling, infiniting. She pushed down hard on the handle and unleashed water everywhere. It tackled her by the legs, forcing her forward like a mob into the yard, then flattened her so it could trample on top and race ahead faster, gathering rage.

Her ears popped when she resurfaced. The front yard was a filthy swamp with random islands of bald dirt rising above opaque sludge. Her clotheslines were still cinched tightly to a tree trunk on one end, but the other drooped, trailing off into the marsh, offering hope and help to whomever might fall in.

It took her almost a minute before she noticed she wasn't alone. Her neighbor, Mrs. Rao, was in her own front yard, soaked to the skin. She was bent over, examining something Isa couldn't make out over the low wall separating their two houses. Isa scratched her own skin. It itched from the flood, lukewarm indoors but cooling now, the wetness not so much crusting on her skin as growing into it, melding and putting down roots.

Mrs. Rao's hair was plastered to her skull, streaks of scalp showing. A drip of water fell from her forehead.

"Texture macam yogurt," she announced as Isa splashed closer, referring to the mud. "Milo yogurt."

"Hmm," Isa assented. She surveyed the damage in her neighbor's yard. A rattan stool with rigid strands unfurled and sticking out like broken springs, and rock-hard sofa squares covered in flowery fabric. An old boom box stranded nearby, a glistening rectangularity.

That night, tossing on a motel bed, Isa dreamed of Gong Gong, strumming an abacus like an instrument, smiling the whole time.

Kuala Lumpur was no London. Hell, come to that, it wasn't even Shanghai or Singapore. Sure it tried hard enough; there were things like Berjaya Times Square, the world's largest something or other built by a French company, and Tribeca Kuala Lumpur, "a contemporary expression of downtown living." Cyberjaya answered to Silicon Valley. But no: it was like buying counterfeit Gucci and Prada, just not the same at all.

At least her sublet was in the heart of this wannabe metropolis. Isa watched a sliver of skyline beckoning between two office towers across the street. Her mother had just called, and Isa had let it go to voice mail. She didn't feel like explaining for the umpteenth time why she'd chosen to move by herself to KL when there was a perfectly fine spare bedroom in her mother's semidetached unit.

"It's just for a while, until they restore my place," Isa'd said.

"How long?"

"One month, maybe two."

"Wah! Must be expensive! How come must take so long?"

"The flood did quite a bit of damage, Mum."

"You won lotto meh? Come stay with me lah! I cook for you!"

But no, Isa had preferred to interpret the flood as a sign. She'd been ready to leave her job anyway. Bigger things awaited, she felt sure of it.

She reached for a laptop on the dining counter, which was positioned only a few feet from the front door. The studio was undeniably small. She planned on living frugally and alone for a while, so the size suited her.

On the laptop's screen was a colorful poster. While exploring KL, she'd seen a paper copy tacked to the trunk of a streetlamp, but that one had been stripped of its vibrant colors by tropical heat and humidity. The poster called, in English and Malay, for a congregation of citizens. It prophesized the biggest peaceful demonstration against governmental corruption and injustice the country had ever seen.

Isa felt vaguely ashamed. She had read in the newspapers about rampant corruption at the top, of course, but living in a small town had somehow removed all urgency from the topic. Taxes kept rising, while the ringgit kept dropping. More and more people had been arrested for dissent (called "sedition" by those in power). In Taiping, these events had seemed as remote and immovable as the mountains, always there, bringing rain or blessing fair weather as they wished. It had never occurred to her that she could do something about it. But now that she was in the heart of the action, she could feel the restless power of the people crackling like static in the air. She wanted to hum along with it, tune into the frequency.

She got up early the day of the protest. She was ready. There was a chicken floss bun in the fridge and a new orange shirt laid out at the foot of the bed. It was hours still until the protest. On the internet, a rumor was going around that the government had ordered a shutdown of LRT and monorail lines. It seemed silly, hoping to thwart protesters by taking away public transportation that was infuriatingly unpredictable to begin with. She sneered. Yeah, that would make angry people shrug and go home all right.

The orange shirt was one she had picked out at random in a pasar malam. It was several shades off from the "official" orange modeled by organizers in posters, really more persimmon than tangerine. But with a bandanna tied around her forehead, there could be no doubt who she was with.

When she was still a secondary school student, then Prime Minister Mahathir Mohamad had vowed that Malaysia would become a developed nation by 2020. She had been impressed back then, awed that one man could make such a grandiose promise and be responsible for dragging a whole nation to the peak in his wake. Now there were only a handful of years left until the deadline, and one dollar from neighboring Singapore was worth more than three ringgit. They were about to default on that mad boast, and Isa realized that there had been nothing wonderful about one man staking a whole country's honor in such a spectacular way. She felt that Mahathir had signed away some inexpressible thing that belonged in part to her. Somehow, it fell upon the citizens to feel sheepishly ashamed.

She chugged a whole cup of coffee and regretted it. What if there were no bathrooms? She might have to hold it in for hours and hours.

One last look at the event invite for walking directions. A mouse scroll brought into view a photo of a sinewy young man. Isa felt a twinge looking at the face of the movement, his hair spiked and his arms crossed. So young. Years younger than she was, and they were calling him the hope of the nation.

Foreign and local commentary alike were predicting crackdowns. If things get desperate, run—that was what she had read in her brief research on what to do during a demonstration.

Outside, it was relatively cool, really quite a nice day for a protest. At least heat stroke was one less thing to worry about. Otherwise there might be more martyrs than expected, suffocated by halos of soaked cheesecloth air and shrouded in auras of sticky, weighty sweat. Isa walked along the edge of a tar road, staying in the shade thrown by tall buildings: banks and business towers and corporate plazas. The streets were unusually deserted. Afraid of looters, shop owners had shuttered their businesses for the day. The weather was so fine, though, that the scene did not seem sinister, nothing like a zombie movie. As she got closer to the designated congregation point, she fell in with others wearing orange, mostly young or middle-aged people of all races, and now and then a senior citizen. At least the seniors all seemed to be with companions, probably neighbors or family. But she'd seen an ad for fortified milk recently that had a CGI depiction of old bones snapping readily. It made Isa worry for them. She looked at one protester, layers of wrinkles barely holding up his cheeks.

Her steps slowed. Somewhere ahead, the vanguard she couldn't see had crawled to a stop. Overhead a helicopter buzzed by. Media? Police? To them the protesters must have looked like an accordion, the center packing into itself as more and more people shuffled in from the two opposite ends of the congregation point. Isa looked at a few people crossing the two-way road toward where she was standing. A sudden impulse made her want to push through the bodies and jostle her way to the middle of the road, onto a narrow divider overgrown with weeds stirring in the breeze. She wanted to skip along the divider, balancing herself, and clear this can of sardines. It could be a shortcut of sorts to the heart of the protest. But too many layers of people hemmed her in. It was probably safer being crushed like this anyway, she thought—strength in numbers. There was no reason for her to feel uneasy.

The crowd inched forward a bit more, and she saw them, the police, standing out in deep navy and some sort of helmet and gas mask combo. The respirator-helmet was bright red, just a little bit orange under the sun's glare. The back of the contraption read "POLIS."

Many protestors looked expectant. Some seemed grim. At least—she looked up at the sky—it certainly would not rain today. Funny that she'd come to inspect clouds so minutely, never having been one of those kids who pretended that clouds looked like dogs or cars or whatever. The clouds looked nothing like anything. They were useful skybound tools that could offer a glimpse of the future.

A speech started somewhere down the road. From the quality of the sound, someone was using a handheld megaphone. Isa stood on tiptoe to see better, but everyone else around was also agitating to be witnesses.

"Demokrasi!" a man close behind her shouted abruptly, interrupting the speech and making her jump. She felt her heart thrum. There were isolated cheers and echoes in response to the outburst, but the majority seemed intent on listening to the unknown speaker. It must be the very young man featured on the poster.

"Tanah tumpahnya darahku!" the voice projected, tinny. "This is the land on which our blood is spilt!"

"Our blood! Yes! Our country!"

Now the full force of the crowd could be heard. Sharp whistles and a blended roar traveled up and down the road, creating such a thick, substantial atmosphere that Isa felt she would be able to crowd surf on top. She was still unconsciously on tiptoe, smiling, not because she wanted to see better, but because she really did feel buoyed. This was right. Everything was right. She was here, and she mattered, and they would have to listen.

She matched every inch gained by those ahead, shuffling her feet along. They all wanted to be closer, hear the young man better.

"Where is our money?" he roared.

"Who gave Leonardo DiCaprio Marlon Brando's Oscar?" he demanded.

"Why does the PM's wife have so many handbags? Whose money paid for Miranda Kerr's jewelry?"

"Ours! Ours! Ours!" everyone chanted.

"Make them explain! This is *our* country, not theirs, no matter what they say. When they say you are not patriotic, you say you are! Because you love Malaysia"—cheers— "you do not tolerate those who are greedy and want to suck the country dry. We love Malaysia! The PM does not love Malaysia!"

"He does not!" screamed the crowd.

"Let's make him explain! Tell us where our money went!" the youth's voice cracked. Isa's heart soared. They would now wind their way through the streets of KL until they reached the royal palace, where they would submit a petition asking the prime minister to step down. They had been assured it was a respectfully worded document.

The procession snaked for maybe three hundred feet, then convulsed. She tripped into the person right ahead. Behind her, the wall of humans started jostling, food atoms in a microwave.

"Hey!" she cried out, shoved off-balance again.

"Merdeka!" someone shouted.

"Merdeka! Merdeka!" Different sections of the crowd picked it up.

"Demokrasi!"

A loudspeaker whinnied from far off, then a different voice came on, not the youth. "Everyone! Friends! Do not provoke. Do not push the police! They are allowing us to walk peacefully to the palace. Stay on the path!"

Smattered booing. Isa tried to keep pace as well as she could, stepping on others' shoes a few times. Suddenly the crowd ahead of her loosened, blank spaces appearing like in a slinky stretched. A cheer rose from behind, then everyone rushed forward, sweeping her along like so much flotsam. She hurried her feet and thought of the flood, feeling suspended in some thick jelly medium, legs paddling uselessly in place. The crowd veered sharply. Then chaos. Some people screamed for them to stop and go back the way they'd come, while others shouted the imperative to push forward and show the country what people power looked like.

When the nets of tear gas whirred over her personal piece of sky, Isa ran. Those who had buoyed her up had scattered. The loudspeaker had ceased; no more instructions from voices high and thin in their effort to carry. She ran blindly and immediately started choking, stumbling onto one knee. She had not cried during the young man's passionate speech, but tears came hard now, government chemicals turning her body on itself.

She was on both knees. *Not fair*, she kept thinking. *My tears are supposed to be for me, to cry for my country swooning to ruins. It shouldn't be like this. I haven't even cried for my father yet.*

A hand hauled her up by one armpit. She sucked in a big gulp of air in surprise and pain. Her body rose, hacking and choking, against her will. She was shuffled lopsided down the street, away from the advancing tear gas trucks. She tried to lift her head to see how far away the enemy loomed. She couldn't; she was puking dry toxic air. A damp shirt met her outstretched hand. Someone gloved her hand with their own and helped clamp the shirt over her nose and mouth. She struggled. The hand became a vise. Soon she realized she felt better. The soggy shirt was acting as a filter, keeping out some of the poisoned air. What was it wet with? Drain water? Rain puddles? Sweat? Spit? Urine?

The trucks closed in. The arc of their discharge sagged and swelled, sagged and swelled, gaining ground. In another moment their ejection would splash over her.

Isa's handler changed directions. They had been limping along the traffic road, taking the same path the trucks took, trying to outrun them. Now they swerved, making a diagonal cut to get off the streets, heading toward a row of shuttered retail shops.

"Help! Tolong! Open!" It was a man holding on to her, and he had a deep voice. Close to her nose, a fist started banging on the shutters of a watch repair shop, the pounding reverberating through her body. She tried to lean less against the man propping her up.

"Please go away . . . I'm just a poor shopkeeper! Please lah, I can't help you!" came the muffled reply through rusty shield-like shutters.

They tried a few more shops, the sound of metal meeting fist punctuating their noisy attempts to breathe. Once, the fist slowed, came off the shutters, and shook itself around like a wet dog. She shrank. The man cursed.

At last a kedai runcit lifted its gate. Isa stumbled in, shoved from behind. The Malay shopkeeper looked at her with pity visible even through tear-blurred eyes.

She was steered toward a plastic stool. "Breathe," a woman whispered. Isa felt a swell of gratitude, and more tears came. "Thank you," she whispered back.

The shopkeeper brought water. She looked up into his face. It was wrinkled at the ends of both eyes, but perfectly smooth everywhere else. She took the shirt off her face and shivered, inexplicably smelling the crispness of a sunny winter morning. She scanned faces to find the one who had gotten her away. A man, thin limbs, thick square eyebrows, nodded. Isa offered the shirt to him.

"It's not mine," he said.

Isa knew she was lucky. There had been arrests at the protest, people roughed up. The authorities had managed to sink their claws into the young face of the movement, who'd been held for days, then unceremoniously released. Since then, there had been no word from him, which was unusual. The movement issued statements saying he was recovering, but word on the internet was that the police had broken him, snapped his spirit like fragile old bones.

Isa wondered what had been done to him. She imagined beatings, psychological tortures, and threats. Would she have held up in his place? How long? She tried to imagine, measuring her own worth. Which was the one that had gotten to him, physical or psychological?

She felt surer about withstanding any mind tricks they might play on her, so it would probably be something physical that would make her succumb. But she had read that women could bear much more pain than men could. On the other hand, there were things, physical things, which could be done to women that were not usually done to men.

Isa shuddered. She abandoned the thought exercise and got up for water and food. Her throat felt forever parched these days.

Carefully, she spread open a greasy bundle of newspaper and banana leaf to reveal the nasi lemak wrapped within.

Then she groped for her mouse and nudged the coconut rice aside to make way for navigation. She'd started feeling paranoid out there alone, so here she was, in the safety of her own place, ready to learn more about the secrets her government was keeping from her.

She clicked on five articles, started four, and finished one. They were all about a recent scandal that would have made Malaysia, once again, an international laughing-stock, if only the international community actually cared enough about the country to pay attention. The Federal Court had reaffirmed Anwar's sodomy conviction. It was ridiculous! Amazing enough that they had gotten away with locking up a deputy prime minister and opposition party leader for six years—six years!—over a charge like *unnatural sex*, of all things! Now it seemed there was a legion of shadowy, disposable young men waiting in the wings, ready to emerge, spread themselves wide, and swear, hand on Quran, that they had been sodomized by Anwar, thus giving the government another excuse to throw Anwar in jail. It would never end! They had found the perfect "crime," one that could never be conclusively proven but that could be used to jail someone on the weight of false testimony alone, time and again.

Isa heaved an oily sigh. Even that hurt, air sanding down her windpipe. She refreshed the news page, wanting the distraction of new outrage. The page loaded in fits, and before it was even done she'd caught two words that made her feel like her heart was making a run for it through her bowels. What was this? "Isa Sin," her name. Why was she a top featured article? Frantic flashbacks to the day of the protest brought no answers—she had not done anything to draw attention to herself; as far as protesters went she had been average, even subpar, needing the help of others to escape the tear gas trucks. She had not incited anyone. The only sounds she had made were gasps for air. She hadn't been one of those leading charges against fences of policemen either. What could it be? "Poems." "Inflammatory." "Pornographic." Even during the protest she had not felt such fear. It bloated her brain, pushing it against her skull. How did they know she used to write poetry?

Under a picture of Anwar's care-lined face were two poems:

Let's Talk About Sodomy
  By Isa Sin

How it always starts:
something goes in,
something else comes out.

Jail, I mean.
A change of clothes,
a change of goals,
a change of souls.

Would you?
If you could self
-inflict a white eye.

Wide-eyed, we learn how
bellies belie
anus' onus,
how
semen in seams of men,
of mattress, matters

in court, of course.
The evidence, strained,
not as if through a sieve,
but meaning tough to conceive.

We case a building
where they are
building a building
because we are
building our case.

Let's talk. Just
Yes or No,
Please.

Let's Talk About Sodomy II
　　By Isa Sin

There is always a sequel;
truth lies in repetition.

Re-dig ridic relics.
Those who do not learn from the lessons of
history are condemned to repeat its mistakes, ha haha.
What century are we in anyway?

Your Lordship has lied.

Seriously, can't you control your own lordship a little
better?
It's bad enough we have to take seriously
the application of the penal code

toward penile penetration.
It's almost as bad as arguing that
"anal canal" rhymes.

Let's talk, I go.
You can can it, you say.
"Can I fuck you today?" the nation is asked.
But
there was still light filtering through the curtains.

Already there were over a thousand comments, most of
them simple "likes" and thumbs-up icons accompanied by
digital laughter. Interspersed were expressions of disgust
and speeches about declining morals. Isa's hand slipped off
her mouse. Her palm was wet. Half-consciously she lifted
it to cover her mouth, then grimaced as the film of sweat
stuck, transferred to her face.

An arrhythmic pounding startled her. She jerked up.
Some part of her cracked, maybe a shoulder. The door handle
rattled violently. The overlapping knocks and the energetic
vibrations of the handle told her there was more than
one person beyond. It wasn't a friend, and it wasn't anyone
next door. It must be—

"Polis!"

She wanted to shout above the din that she was here,
so that they would stop the assault on her door. But even
the banging had a forceful authority of its own, and it
muted her. She hurried across the living room, noticing
on her way that one of the prints hanging on the wall was
crooked. As soon as the door swung open they stomped
into her apartment. She had barely time to scuttle aside
and avoid contact. Dimly she congratulated herself also
on her perspicacity, for it *was* the police, standing around

her space in heavy boots—she *knew* it—and scanning rooms to find—what? Whom? Her heart roiled.

"You are detained under the Internal Security Act."

She registered that the shortest man seemed to be in charge. He seemed gentle enough as he put a guiding hand between her shoulder blades and steered her deeper into the apartment. She made out that she was supposed to pack one change of clothes. As she walked out of the living area, she saw from the corner of her eye that the other taller policemen were rifling through the printouts near her computer, all of which were about some form or another of the government's wrongdoing.

"What am I being arrested for?" she asked, though she knew.

She couldn't find her duffle bag. Impatient, the short policeman shook out a Giant supermarket plastic bag from the kitchen and ordered her to put her clothes into the bag. She blushed, trying her best to sandwich her bra and panties in between a T-shirt and a pair of artificially distressed black jeans. A different policeman stood nearby, shaking his head, his face mournful. Isa did not understand what was intended by his emotive gesture. She looked at him inquiringly, pleadingly. He produced a pair of handcuffs.

Meanwhile, over a hundred miles away in Taiping, residents were locking their gates and staying indoors. A tiger had escaped from the zoo, which was located smack in the heart of town. Visitors had been ordered to evacuate the zoo, and no one knew where the tiger was. The animal had cleared nearly six feet of wall in a single bound, because the commotion of a citizen's protest nearby drove it mad, and it could bear the cacophony no more.

o

Isa's throat burned more than ever. She had not been given water for hours—how many she didn't know because they had left her alone in the back of a truck. At least they had uncuffed her. With no windows, it had been impossible to follow the turns and pauses she had felt the truck make on its journey. They could be one, two, three states away by now, for all she knew. But it seemed clear that she had not been brought to a police station, for there was one just a few streets away from her apartment, and it would not have taken nearly as long to get there. If she had to guess, she would say that it was one of the silent hours just before sunrise.

There had been a female officer in uniform waiting in the back of the truck when they herded her in. Twice during the dark journey, Isa tried to engage this woman, but Isa's voice was still weak and easy to ignore. After the second attempt, Isa started crying. That was when the short policeman had leaned over and uncuffed her, so she could swipe at her face.

She suddenly yearned for the Giant plastic bag that contained her clothes. She felt around for it with her hands and feet. No. No. Emptiness. Air. Her heart roiled again. They had taken it away.

The double doors of the truck swung outward. Isa made no move to get up until her eyes had adjusted. She peered. Four men and a woman materialized, waiting for her. The woman was the same one who had made the journey with Isa. There was a giant mole on the officer's right cheek, a mound of matte on an otherwise porous surface. Isa hadn't noticed it back in the truck's blindfold of boxy darkness.

She duckwalked to the rim of the truck and extended one leg, but the woman with the mole shooed her back in, punching her fists aggressively forward.

"Please," Isa begged. "No need to cuff me. Tak payahlah, puan, tuan. I'm not going to run away."

The woman clucked her tongue and grabbed Isa's hands. Behind her, an officer Isa had not seen before met her eyes. She turned away, scared.

The truck was parked only a few feet away from a building entrance, which opened up into a room with lights that were too bright for her. She blinked her scrunched-up eyes as they flanked her forward.

"Where is this?"

"Police Remand Center." Isa wished she didn't have to cough so badly. What was a "remand"?

"Please, water."

This time no one seemed to have heard her. She lifted her head and realized that it had been bowed all this while, and all she had seen of the room was its blank cement floor. She chastised herself and made a mental note to be observant. She should be scrutinizing any and all details. It seemed like an important thing to do in her situation.

The room was fluorescent ceiling lights, yellow once-white walls, one single small window, and uniformed bodies occupying spaces where furniture should be. She was estimating the room's dimensions when the female officer came up, tapped her arm, and then was propelling her by her elbow down a hallway that branched from the main space they were just in.

Doors appeared on both sides of the hallway. Immediately, Isa saw the lone open door waiting for her near the end, before the hallway became part of a T-junction. Fear that had been numbed to a pause now came back in a strong burst, like yet another wave of fireworks when a lull had seemed to signal the end.

She must have slowed because the woman was wrenching her elbow forward. Isa listed and involuntarily remembered the protest, when she had also been lopsided, hauled along by her armpit. She shook.

Staring at her, waiting in the room, were one tall man and two other women. There was a single wooden chair, but no one sat on it. The tall man had a plain, nondescript face forming the backdrop for an impressive mustache. He spoke first, telling the woman with the mole to uncuff Isa.

She rubbed her wrists together and looked from one strange face to the next, her subconscious inventing hope by having her pick out the person most likely to help her. Perhaps the petite woman in a tudung, whose lips looked soft and sympathetic? She looked out of place here, more like a kindergarten teacher.

"Please, water," Isa repeated. Her stomach flared when the woman with soft lips was indeed the one who moved, walking out of her field of vision, then returning with a bottle of Spritzer.

The water was oddly warm, like it had been sitting out in the sun, but of course it was still night, dumb and dark.

"Take off your clothes," the tall man ordered while the bottle of water was still tilted, sloping into her mouth. Isa choked and sputtered water down her shirt and jeans.

The tall man sneered.

"Please," she begged.

"Please what? Oh, don't worry, I'm not interested in your body, I like pretty women only, not ugly ones like you," he laughed.

Isa trained her eyes in turn on the women in the room, but none of them had any expression on their faces. When the woman with the mole advanced a step, Isa knew that the reason they were present was to help strip her. She grabbed hold of the hem of her shirt.

"I want a lawyer, a lawyer."

The man laughed again.

"Lawyer-lawyer semua still sleeping lah, ah moi. Come on ah moi, don't be shy, I already said you are too ugly for me. Look at you! Everything flat. Eyes dirty color. Macam mongrel. You want me to close my eyes? Okay I close my eyes." He shut his eyes, but immediately opened them again. "See? I close my eyes when you take off your clothes."

"Why?" she cried, nonsensical.

A hand touched the skin of her arm. She shrieked.

"I'll do it myself!" she sobbed.

"Good girl," said the man.

She pulled her shirt upward, moving as slowly as possible, and then suddenly yanked the whole thing off in one move, afraid somehow that by undressing slowly it would look like a striptease. She held her shirt in a fist by her side until the woman with soft lips came and took it from her.

The man's eyes were not closed, but he was making a show of staring at a corner of the ceiling. Isa looked up. In that corner was a water stain and, nearby, a black arrow pointing to Mecca.

She stepped out of her jeans and looked helplessly at the woman with soft lips. From behind her, she sensed the woman with the mole coming.

The man started up again: "Rilek lah ah moi. You must have shown your body to lots and lots of guys, right? I know you enjoy different-different men. You look like that kind of woman. So this is nothing special, right?"

"Please," she begged, this time looking at no one, at the wall in front of her. "Let me keep my underwear."

The woman with the mole stepped behind Isa and

unclasped her bra, but pinched the two halves together until Isa surrendered, raising her own hands to take over. "It's okay," the woman whispered, very softly. Her voice was unexpectedly high and childlike.

The women half pulled, half nudged Isa out the door, naked. Then she lost control, howling and struggling with them as they marched her down a different hallway, feeling it harder and harder to breathe as her sobs became hiccups, ignoring remonstrations that if she did not stop making so much noise she would wake the male inmates and then they would see her buck naked; did she really want that?

After a while, they were in front of what was obviously a jail cell of some kind. The fight had gone out of her for the last hundred feet or so, and she could barely hold herself upright when suddenly, in synchrony, the women's hands and arms left her body. They retreated out of sight, and Isa was left tottering in front of the open cell. What did they want her to do? Did they mean to complete her humiliation by having her walk, tame and docile, into her own cage? She was about to turn around and face her abusers when she was kicked in the buttocks with great force. She fell forward and her left cheek hit the hard floor first, followed by her sprawled arms and then the rest of her body, the impact vibrating through her gut, her bare ass laid out on view.

She braced, but no one laughed.

When day broke, she could see enough to distinguish a tiny barred opening high off the ground. It did not deserve the name of "window." Her hand shuffled forward, and she worried the sharp edge of the cement platform on which she lay. It was obviously meant to be slept on, this cold dais, for they had placed on it a thin cotton blanket and a pillow that felt like it was stuffed with plastic straws. She could choose between sleeping on the blanket to counteract some of the cement's harshness and hiding her naked body under the thing.

She had not slept, not really. The "bed" grew out of the wall like a rigid tumor. Lying down, she had found it was too short for her, even though she was only five four. She curled up. Some time ago she had almost drifted off, exhausted, when she thought she heard a knock come from the wall right next to her. She jolted, banging her shin hard against the platform. Was it a friend, a fellow inmate unfairly detained without trial? Or more likely than not it was a trick they must be playing on her, preventing her from getting sleep, trying to confuse her or get her hopes up. *Oh god*, she thought. Who would miss her? Surely someone would do something for her, out there? Think, think on the bright side. Maybe her mother was getting help at that very moment.

And that was enough to bring back a memory she had suppressed for years.

When she was nine, her mother had caught her with fruit stolen from their neighbor's tree. Young Isa defended herself, explaining that although the guava tree had roots stemming from the neighbor's compound, its branches stuck their way over the fence into what was technically *their* house, so it wasn't really stealing, right?

For this bit of talking back, her mother had made her wait in the living room while she went off to fetch a rattan cane. When she came back, she instructed Isa to display her right palm, holding it outstretched and faceup. Then her mother showed her how to steady the upturned palm by encircling her left fingers in a tight grip around her right wrist, and even helpfully demonstrated this offering of the right palm by the left to prevent the diving board effect.

The diving board effect, her mother went on to explain, happened when the cane came whipping down on the palm and the palm could not withstand the force, thus drooping to an angle that made it cumbersome to deliver the next strike, and the next, and the one after that, without unnecessary delay. It was more efficient if Isa used both hands to support the target palm and keep it horizontal. Then it would be over quicker.

It began. After about ten strokes, both hands started their descent toward the ground anyway, and her mother, impatient, clucked for her to turn around. As soon as Isa's back was to her mother, the tears flowed. Before Isa had time to feel a smidgen of pride at keeping them unseen, she was wailing hysterically against her will. But she did what she was told well enough despite the crying, lifting up her pinafore and holding hands out at her sides, a fistful of fabric in each. The hem pressed into her right palm and it burned.

Now the cane came down again and again, and she could not see its arc to brace herself. Her knees quaked. There was a horrible crunching sound, and her first thought was that her mother had broken her bones. But it was only the rattan cane snapping in half.

Breakfast slid through a slot was two pieces of toast with a pat of margarine. One of them was an endpiece, something she used to despise and always tossed into the trash when she was living free. There was also lukewarm Milo in a deformed tin mug that looked like it had been used to bash someone's head in. No spoon.

Rallying after food, she reminded herself to be observant. She got up and wrapped the thin blanket around herself, as if she were on her way to a relaxing hot tub. The material had long ceased to be scratchy, sometime shortly after dawn.

She paced. Her cell was tiny, about twelve Isa feet by fifteen Isa feet, although her feet were not very large, so maybe the actual measurements were closer to—nine by twelve? The cement dais was maybe five by four real feet, but it loomed, looking like it took up most of the cell's space. No, she would not think about human sacrifices.

"My name is Isabella Sin," she murmured. She had read that prisoners kept in isolation often lost their minds. "I am twenty-eight. I thought I was a writer, then I thought I wasn't, but now I know I am."

"Take off the blanket. Squat."—were the orders.

She started to plead again, but remembered from a few hours ago that it just made them crueler. She did as told. Her labia parted and it felt cold, down there. She tried to draw her knees closer together and almost toppled over. She hadn't realized that she felt dizzy.

A man in uniform stood just outside her cell. The door was open, but she knew he counted on her nudity to keep her in place. Unfamiliar. A different man. How did they all possess the same grim coldness?

"Get up. Follow me."

"Why?" she asked. She meant the pointlessness of making her squat.

"You're leaving" was the reply.

She was led to a bathroom. It had a small mirror clouded unevenly at the edges with dirt and hung too high off the ground for her. While washing her hands, the tears came again. After some indecision, she pushed herself up on tiptoes. The glass was too dirty for a good look, but she knew—the eye bags were there, and the fucked-up hair, and the scratches on the cheek that had made contact with cell floor. Her nose itched. She sneezed, then realized she had not bothered to close her mouth, a behavior she had condemned in others—like peasants and rural folk. Fear came again like a gust to blow off the leaves of her sanity one by one. *My name is Isabella Sin!*

After the bathroom, she was led back to the room from yesterday. She drew a few ragged breaths and tried to brace herself for more humiliation. But the man did not follow her into the room. When she turned to look, she saw he had closed the door on her. She was alone again.

There was that same lone wooden chair. Her clothes were in a pile on the floor. She bent over, picked her clothes up, and shook them out. They were the ones she had taken off in this room. The change of clothes she had been told to pack was nowhere to be seen. Who knew what they were holding it for?

After dressing, she stood next to the chair, waiting, until the door opened and the woman with soft lips came in, looking haggard. She sighed when she saw Isa.

"Follow me," the woman said.

There was a brief brilliance of sunshine, bright shadows patterning the ground, before Isa was put in the back of another Black Maria. She saw that there was the same number of guards with her. Someone shut the door, and it was darkness once more. The engine started and rumbled, then quieted as they coasted away. The people with her were silent bodies moving only when swayed by the truck's journey.

Some period of time later, she looked at nothing in particular and said, "I didn't write those poems." She did not expect a response. But one came, from the shadowy figure sitting closest to the driver's seat: "You're just like the boy before you. Brave to act but chicken to admit. Why call yourself activist if you don't dare accept the consequences?"

She thought about the face of the movement. So he had recanted, or somehow given in. *Pantomine. No. Palindrome? Wrong.* She worried at her memory until it came to her, the word she had learned so many years ago: *Palinode.* She closed her eyes, doubling the darkness, tripling the night. That was what she felt to be outside, beyond the truck: night.

My name is Isabella. This is my country. Its name is Malaysia.

She should have thought of it earlier. She didn't know why she hadn't. Yet another leaf lost, blown into space and then abandoned to the ground.

Not too long before the Black Maria came to an idle, she had smelled familiar rain. Foolishly, she had been comforted by this proof that she retained her "skills" yet.

"It's going to rain," she said out loud. This time no one responded.

Soon, pattering could be heard against the vehicle's roof. An occasional ping sounded against the sides as well, drops angled by wind.

Now, stumbling out onto gray earth, she knew that she had been brought to the infamous Kamunting Detention Centre, where most of the Internal Security Act detainees were held. She had recognized the rain even in darkness because it was *her* rain. Kamunting was a short ten-minute drive from Taiping—in fact, they must have driven through her town to get here—perhaps they had even rumbled right past her own house!

Cruel, cruel! She shook her head vigorously. When a hand touched her she sprang her head upward and saw, written overhead at the entrance of the prison camp, the words NEGARA KITA TANGGUNGJAWAB KITA.

"*Our* country, *our* responsibility." The pronoun, *kita*, was inclusive of addressees, referencing a burden shared. She wondered why they had not used the exclusive pronoun instead: NEGARA KAMI TANGGUNGJAWAB KAMI.

"*Our* country (not yours), *our* responsibility (not yours)." We've got this. Stay out of our way.

She lost consciousness for a microsecond, then regained reality and remained standing, handcuffed, her jeans sticking to her from pooled sweat.

The nation was in an uproar over the midnight raid and arrest of Isabella Sin, coming so soon on the heels of a massive demonstration that had felt like a victory for the people. But already the news had engendered plans for further protests, this time calling for her release.

Reporters were told that Ms. Sin had been detained without trial for good reasons: for sedition and for disrupting racial harmony—that delicate, neurotic thing only the government had expertise to feed and grow. After being disappeared, Isabella Sin was not heard from again for what felt like a very long time.

THE OLYMPIAN

Half moon, around four months pregnant
He came to me again tonight. I brimmed with victory. It is because I have the best butt, I know. Not to be crass. Let the other women sneer about the "unknown origins" of my proudest feature, so unusual among people of our kind. I was chosen because I was blessed by God, who protects our great country, Him, and all the rest of us.

I dressed and strolled slowly to breakfast. My eyes had been a little puffy in the hand mirror, but the color was high and fresh in my cheeks. My left arm felt sore. I believe it has something to do with little tears that are created in my muscles during physical activity, but I cannot remember the relevant facts.

I wish again that I could borrow a book. It's getting harder and harder to remember what I'd learned in classrooms, sitting on rows of rickety wooden benches. It seems such a long time ago now. The benches were old and rickety on purpose, I remember thinking, so that when our attentions drifted and we shook our legs in boredom, the benches would creak and give us away to the teachers. I was such a child then, afraid only of an adult's admonishment, not realizing that there are so many other things in life.

The corridor that leads to the dining room is long and straight. When the wind huffs, as it did this morning, it comes whistling down an unerring line straight at you, as if personally seeking you out. I put my hand out to graze a thick, round pillar as I walked past, shivering at the marble's chill.

It's getting harder to remember my family's faces too. As I walked to breakfast, I cycled through them all again, one by one, practicing memory: Father, Mother, Brother. Father, Mother, Brother.

Knife moon, around two months pregnant
I'm leaning back on the bed writing this entry, waiting for Him. The bedding is soft, and I feel sunken and snug. I think about Father wrapping towels around his hot jugs of liquor before picking them up. I'd asked him once, why not just wait until it cools down? He'd shaken his head and laughed, replying that old men have no patience.

You're not old, I remember correcting. In response, he'd given his head a few more wags.

I caught my thighs jiggling. How did this happen? I gave the right one a slap, willed it to be still. I am failing to possess mental fortitude. Divine Leader, He said our enemies halfway across the globe are like this, scatterbrained and always led by the nose by meaningless trivialities. He says this is because they are all addicted to cell phones that they carry around wherever they go. The mini computers entertain them and think for them, and slowly our enemies' brains deteriorate due to misuse. That is our opening, He said. If we can retain the nimbleness of our thoughts and the independence of our brains, without aid of machines, then we will remain human and in possession of our awesome mental faculties, while the enemies devolve into babies who cannot function without being told what to do by lifeless computers.

Now I'm yawning, too. Another sign of weakness: boredom. Although the hour is getting late. To keep my mind sharp, I will try to invent new stories about my world. I'll find an interesting object here in my room. Curtain, robe, couch: so many things in here are soft.

I get up to stand in front of the window. I see, high in the sky, something cold and hard: the knife moon sharp as a scabbard. She is my favorite, the one upon which many stories have been built. My current best has her getting pregnant all the time, giving birth to stars, her consecutive children, one after another without pause. This is because she is lonely, untouchably without peer in the night. But the stars she makes surround her, winking in joy, and this soothes her.

I think this is a pretty story.

A memory just burrowed to the surface, like one of the worms in the sandy part of the royal pleasure garden, appearing out of nowhere on an afternoon so sunny you squint and think the wriggling might just be a spot in your vision.

In the memory, Mother has her back to me, chopping green onions. I am boasting, describing to her how my teacher had called me up to stand in front of the whole class earlier that morning. "This girl has written an excellent essay that is in great harmony with the virtues we all should strive to live by. Let her be your example. Purify your thoughts, strain out unclean ideas, and work hard to record the triumph of your mind down on paper, so others may benefit."

I told Mother how much I had wanted to grin, but how

I'd managed to suppress it, because I knew I should be humble and dignified. I paused, expecting Mother to turn around with a big smile and put her warm palms against my cheeks. But the "tok tok" of the knife against bamboo board went on.

"I fear you will be just smart enough to know the truth of your situation, but not smart enough to escape it," Mother said.

I must have fallen asleep earlier. I am frightened by this. What if Divine Leader had come for me, seen me fail at my station, and left for another? Or worse, perhaps he had not come at all.

In the hand mirror my hair is squashed against my cheeks, the top of one ear peeking out unattractively. And oh, the beginnings of wrinkles are bunched up below my eyes. Ah, I am old, I have served Divine Leader for five years; soon there will be tear-filled pouches dragging the corners of my eyes down. He did not come for me because I am losing my looks.

I stand as straight as I can. Maneuvering the hand mirror as I have done countless mornings, I examine my bottom. The arc formed by the small of my back seems as dramatic as ever—like a cove carved by patient ocean waves over many moons, Divine Leader had once said, swooping with his palm. I crane my neck and look harder. The fleshy halves themselves seem to have distorted over-night, like sacks of plucked cotton left out in a thunderstorm. I press my fingers gingerly into a buttock. As I feared, the give is different, like loose flour, whereas before it was like the best baked bread.

My body is changing, as Mother had warned it would. I am afraid to think of what comes next.

o

Spring Flower smirked as soon as my shadow crossed the threshold of the dining hall. She clattered her tea cup onto the table so that the other women looked up and also noticed the spectacle: me. I stood tall, summoning all the good thoughts that would help me see this situation in the right light. One, we are all here to serve Divine Leader. Therefore, none of us are better than the others; we are all equal before God and Him. Two, any small way in which I am able to serve this great nation is a wonderful honor. Even if my usefulness is fleeting, I must cherish my duty while it lasts.

My duty. This is the part that is hazy. Before Divine Leader, my duty was to stay chaste, such that I could fulfill my more important, ultimate duty of being a faithful wife. But now I am neither girl nor wife. Will I ever be a wife?

I thought about Divine Leader's wife. I saw her walk by once, regal in soft but vibrant silks, satiny hair piled higher than her own hands could have arranged. Guards surrounding her, she'd nodded when we bowed in her general direction, none of us wishing to draw her attention. I remember feeling oddly shameful for some reason I didn't understand.

Full moon, water breaking
I've sat up long past the time He would have come. From time to time I stood at the window to look at the moon. Tonight I am too downcast to invent tales, so I revisit one my brother told me what seems like a long time ago. I am writing it down before it, too, is forgotten.

Once upon a time, in a place far away, there ruled a cruel tyrant. He waged wars at whim and demanded the best of everything for himself. In that way, he snatched a beautiful young girl away from her poor family and made her his wife. Thanks to her sweet nature, the tyrant was almost happy for a while. The land knew peace and was thankful for it. But one day, a traveling shaman prostrated himself before the tyrant and spoke of an immortality pill hidden somewhere in the realm. This immediately became the tyrant's obsession. He dispatched his men and forced commoners to abandon their livelihoods in search of this pill. Hell bent on attaining everlasting life, he punished those who inevitably came back empty-handed and trembling, his savage streak worsening.

Until one day, soldiers interrupted the tyrant's daily banquet with news that the pill had been found buried deep underground, nestled among the crisscrossing branches of a very old fig tree. The tyrant roared with delight. At last, he would forever continue enjoying this life that yielded such pleasures to him: food from land, sky, and sea; treasures from the four corners of the map. He laughed and ordered more food and drink to be consumed as celebration.

When the first troupe of dancers was worn out, the tyrant ordered a fresh wave. The tyrant's wife retired to her chambers. As quietly as she could, she barred the door from inside and hoped the guards posted outside had not heard. From inside her robe's long sleeve she extracted the pill of immortality, pilfered from the tyrant while he was cursing the flagging dancers. She pondered the tiny pill between her slender fingers, thinking of all the injustice and suffering that would continue unfolding through the ages should her husband indeed never die. She thought about the poor of the land, scraping by at the mercy of one man, without even the hope of one day seeing a more benevolent ruler guide their lives. She had to do something. The tyrant had to be stopped.

The tyrant's wife made up her mind. Her fist tightened around the tiny globe. She took a deep breath and swallowed the pill. At first she felt no different. Then, to her surprise, her body grew lighter and lighter. Gasping, she clung to the foot of the bed, but it was no good. A force, gentle yet supremely strong, buoyed her away from the floor and out the window. As she floated away from earth she cried her goodbyes to her family, hoping they would hear her. Up and up she went, becoming lighter than air, until she reached the moon. There she landed, and there she stayed, the beautiful woman in the moon.

The sun has risen, but the moon can still be seen, hovering around vision's edges, clinging on for as long as she can. I haven't slept. I stand up from the bed to stretch. My shoulders feel pain, and my bones seem to have rusted.

I know I must be strong. I must do better. I want to think of courageous examples to follow, but my mind is tired, I know it. I do not have an excuse for what I thought earlier. It's a story, just a rumor really, of a girl my age who had run away from this divine country, nobody knew why. It seemed she had been poisoned by the enemy's propaganda. Defected, they called it. I thought it an apt word; she must have contained a defect within her to abandon leader, country, and family like that. It could not have been a spontaneous mistake. She had trekked across a long desert and bribed help along the way with her family's valuables, in entirety, strapped to her back. At the end of her journey . . .

That is where I cut the bad thought off. I am writing this down to help me remember my mistake. I must not be selfish; I must not let my little fate interfere with the larger mission of our divine country. I resolve to do my best in my own way. To start, I will not sit anymore. I suspect sitting around for most hours of the day has squashed my bottom into a less desirable shape. Therefore, starting now, I will stand. With luck, my body will find its way back to its true, intended form.

I pick up the hand mirror and smile into it, nodding. Another memory came then, as if sensing my weakness. It was my last dinner at home, the night before I was to be escorted to the royal residence, right here, where I sit and breathe. Back then this place had seemed unreal, impossibly far away. I felt as if I were about to die, then reincarnated into a palace. Mother had made my favorite dish: root vegetables marinated in soy. It was a joyous occasion, but everyone was silent until Father cleared his throat and said, "It is the greatest honor conferred upon us to have you chosen to serve our Divine Leader." As he finished this declaration he glanced at our door and window. I followed his gaze but saw nothing unusual. When I looked back at him, his eyes were red. He resumed describing how proud he was.

Bun moon, around seven months pregnant
Well, I have finally done it. Today, for the first time, I went all day without sitting, from the moment I woke up until now, late at night.

I can't say this achievement has helped me regain Divine Leader's affection. It has certainly invited scorn from the other women, who think I am slowly losing my mind. I have taken to wandering the royal pleasure garden more frequently, because keeping my legs in motion is easier than standing still like a pillar when the afternoon wears on and my legs become tired. My garden strolls confuse the other women. They all avoid the sun like the plague because they do not want their skin to darken. Me, I like to focus on one thing at a time. It gives me purpose to stand as straight as I can for as long as I am able. So that is what I do. Even at the expense of having porcelain skin, which, if I am honest, I will never attain anyway.

I am sitting on the bed now, massaging my calves. It feels good. Feels like a better kind of failure, compared to my earlier ones. I can't explain it well.

Spider thread moon, newborn star
I cannot possibly write down the emotions I am experiencing. Today has been a spinning-top kind of day, and now the string has been entirely unraveled, and I am ready to topple onto one side.

Lunch was pleasant. The other women lethargically pecked at their ginseng broth while I had seconds, hoping the extra nutrition would go straight to my bottom. I stood at the vast dining table, towering over everyone else seated. They teased me, of course, but I did not mind. Divine Leader was almost never present at midday meals, and anyway, I was beginning to see results from no longer sitting.

After lunch I smoothed down my clothes and set off into the pleasure garden. These walks had become almost a habit by now, so I was not paying too much attention to my surroundings, beautiful though the shrubberies and artful stone sculptures were.

Suddenly my name boomed from a distance behind me. I whirled, joy and terror intermingled. The voice belonged to Divine Leader; I could not be mistaken. And indeed there he strode, his hands crossed behind his back. Next to him was a tall, thin man, who, though he was keeping pace with Divine Leader, looked as if he was not moving his limbs at all. He seemed to *glide*.

I minced toward them, going as fast as I could while still preserving grace. I stopped at two bows' distance of Divine Leader and sank my head low.

"This is the one," Divine Leader said, amusement in his tone. I kept my forehead level to the ground but raised my lashes. The men appeared to be inspecting me with interest.

"Lift your head," Divine Leader commanded. I swung up. Searching for somewhere to safely land my vision, I focused at random on the other man's collarbone, a sharp slice peeking out of his shirt like a half-concealed weapon.

"Indeed, she stands as straight and still as they say," the man commented.

"All of my pleasure girls have interesting personalities," Divine Leader said. "No two alike."

"Let us put her to a test."

"What do you have in mind?"

"An excuse to perform for you again, Divine Leader." The man smiled, lips thin as my favorite knife moon.

Divine Leader threw back his head and laughed, neck folds creasing.

"This is your lucky day," he said to me. "This man is a national hero. Fifteen years ago, he brought much honor to us by winning an Olympic medal, right on enemy territory. He showed the world that we are not to be disrespected. Pay tribute, girl."

I bowed deep, looking at the Olympian's shoes and wondering what sport had been his mastery. He did not look athletic at all, with his malnourished, skinny frame.

When I arced back through air to face them again, the Olympian jutted his bony chin toward something behind me. "That pine tree," he said. I turned and looked. It was a good fifty feet away, set back from the winding brick path designed for ambling. The tree's feet were crowned by a half ring of boat orchids.

"Go stand under the tree, nice and straight just like you are now. Do not move once you get there."

I bowed and started off toward the tree, wondering about the odd request. Perhaps they would take some photographs of me. It was a fine, clear day, barely any clouds. The natural lighting was good.

I reached the tree and stopped. Up close, its bark was much rougher than it had seemed from my earlier distance. I turned to face Divine Leader and the Olympian.

The Olympian's eyes had disappeared. One eye was squeezed tight. In place of the other was a gaping, bottomless well, tunneling out of his face.

I gasped and winced. The Olympian lowered the rifle he had been aiming at me.

"I said, 'Do not move,' did I not?" he shouted across the manicured lawn.

I bowed in apology, terrified. Out of the corner of my eye I saw embroidered shoes padding toward me. I straightened up and met Spring Flower's eyes. She looked somber, which darkened my terror.

She lifted one hand and revealed a peach, blushing ripe. After a heartbeat's hesitation, she stood on tiptoe and balanced the peach on my head. I caught myself just in time; I'd almost slumped forward so she could have better access.

"Sweet Rain," she whispered, hesitantly letting both hands go. Then she left me.

I looked right ahead, at the Olympian and into his rifle's eye. I did not have a choice. I was locked into this posture, my neck stretching, my soles rooting. A breeze picked up.

I felt a stray strand of hair brush against the very tip of my nose. I shivered against my will.

The Olympian lowered his rifle once more, clearly disappointed at my disobedience. I fought to not close my eyes against the images that rushed me while I stood helplessly still: Father, Mother, Brother; rain swishing through leaks in the roof; Baby, taken from inside me while I slept a drugged sleep; the blood that came month after month.

"What's wrong?" Divine Leader asked, impatient.

"Just a speck of dust," the Olympian replied, nodding respectfully. "I'm sorry to make you wait, Divine Leader." From his pocket he withdrew what looked like a rag and applied it to his gun's crater. I stared, tears almost coming. He had seen me twitch; I knew he had. But he was not giving me away. I compressed my body, willing every muscle to adhere, trying to be both tall and compact at the same time.

The Olympian cradled his gun and slowly brought it up to his face again. He adjusted his aim with a few minute movements, then stood completely still, the dark eye unmoving yet simultaneously reaching for me.

Sweat sprouted near my ears. I clenched my entire being into myself, matching the Olympian as best I could. It seemed that was the true challenge, a test of immobility between us. Until a firecracker went off, and an arrow of air whipped past my crown. I allowed myself the tiniest adjustment; I bit my lip.

"Ahh!" Divine Leader shouted, his voice full of triumph. "Wonderful! I see you have not lost your skills one bit."

The Olympian tapped his rifle against one thigh. He might have been smiling, although it was hard to see from where I stood, with a humming in my ears.

He set out in my direction, gun swinging casually. Divine

Leader seemed taken aback, but he followed the Olympian.

"Now you can move," he said when we were face to face. I swallowed hard but did not relax any part of me. Suddenly, the Olympian bent and carefully placed his gun on the grass, not far from my feet. He rose just to dip immediately into a deep bow.

"Divine Leader, if I may, I would like to present you with a proposal that will bring glory to you and all that you rule."

Divine Leader nodded assent. They did not say anything else until they were a distance away, taking small steps, keeping their voices low. I remained standing until my calves spasmed of their own accord. Then I hurried away, taking one last look at the rifle lying in the grass.

Ladle moon

I cannot believe it. I stand with my back to my new room's window, marveling at how different it is from what I have known for the past five years. Everything had been soft or reflective, smooth to the touch, when I had waited night after night for Him. Now, here, the surfaces are dull and coarse, and sharp edges lurk. The wooden bed frame has not been sanded down completely, splintering here and there. I run my fingers across it, seeking the thorns.

He had seemed such an unlikely person to change my life, the Olympian. Coach, he said to call him. Then again, all the ways my life has been diverted have been unexpected, beyond my ken.

I am here to train, so that I may become a competitive sports shooter. *What a strange phrase*, I'd thought when they first explained it to me. Amusement and death rolled into one.

I understand, of course, that this is a very serious matter. Coach explained to me that Divine Leader had been extremely unwilling to part with me, seeing as I am one of his favorites. But in the end, over tea, Coach convinced Him that extraordinary things in one's possession must be shown off to the world in order to truly shine. If kept locked in a box and only taken out for admiration from time to time, even the brightest jewel would gather dust. I nodded along as Coach nodded in imitation of Divine Leader's reaction to this reasoning.

"Why was I chosen?" I asked, half-afraid of the answer.

"Sharp shooters need to have complete control over every finger, every breath," Coach said. "A single tremor, and all is lost. You have the talent of turning yourself to stone. With my help, you may excel."

I must have unconsciously let slip a smile because Coach continued: "You must know that Divine Leader has a condition."

I waited. Up close, Coach's eyes seemed too cloudy for him to be such an expert shooter.

"You must win medals and let the world see what treasures emerge from Divine Leader's guidance. This is especially important," he paused. "On enemy land, outside of our borders."

I bent my neck, signaling understanding.

"If you fail to bring glory, there will be consequences. So, train hard."

I swore I would. Coach turned to leave. At the door, he paused and said, "One more thing. Attaining glory is as much about winning medals as about conducting yourself honorably on foreign soil. You will be given a computer to study geography and the customs of other lands. Use it wisely."

I held my jubilance in until his footsteps had died off. Then I stood, very still, looking at nothing in particular, seeing Father, Mother, Brother, Baby, woman in the moon, defector. For the first time, I did not stop myself from thinking about them. I wondered what each of them were doing at that exact moment in time.

WHEN
STARBUCKS
CAME

When Starbucks finally came to Taiping, that confused place with the infrastructure of a small town and the population size of a city, K. felt that she could now better decide whether to leave H.

All over Taiping there was a festive mood that hung fog-like around the surrounding mountains. At the brand-new Starbucks store a long queue of people spilled onto the street. They took turns holding the front door open as the line advanced. Air-conditioning poured out of the open door.

Looking at her reflection in the glass storefront, K. thought about the arrival of McDonald's years ago, the last time Taiping had been this excited. H. and K. had gone there on their first date, riding on the wave of exhilaration and feeling rather grand. They were young enough for McDonald's to be swanky. Or perhaps it was not their age but where they grew up that made McDonald's swanky; she didn't know.

She didn't know a lot of things, and she was the first to admit it. But here was Starbucks—Taiping was changing—and maybe she should, too.

She saw H. when it was almost her turn to enter through the glass door. He was third in line at the counter, but still staring at the mounted beverage menu intently, indecisive as usual.

Taking one last look, K. stepped out of the line and walked away into the morning heat.

On her way home, she tapped the steering wheel and started listing reasons that might help her make a decision.

REASON: She was older
She was getting older, older than when she'd first fallen in love with him. And she was older than he.

Perhaps not many people cared anymore if the woman was older than the man, but she thought H.'s mother cared.

The first time K. went over as his girlfriend, his mother treated her like a stranger, even though she had essentially grown up under his mother's eyes. His father, on the other hand, acted as if nothing had changed. Their charade reminded K. of her grandfather, who still talked about Malaysia as if it were Malaya, who asked her name every time she visited.

Dinner was two meat dishes and one vegetable dish, H.'s mother's preparations. Throughout dinner the mother coldly answered whatever question K. put forth as small talk, but afterward, doing dishes in the kitchen while the men watched TV, H.'s mother leaned her face close to K.'s, her body rigidly held away, and offered to teach K. how to make H.'s favorite dish. It was supposed to be kangkung with belacan. Months later, curled up in H.'s lap and making small talk, she found out that it was not.

REASON: She had already wasted four good years on him
Rounded up.

Together they had seen many things. They saw McDota, the local rip-off, close down. K. had had her seventh birthday party there; there was a picture of little K. pushing little

80

H. away from her cake, an old-style picture with rounded corners tucked into a yellow Kodak album kept in a drawer in K.'s house.

K. knew it was her seventh birthday because of the candles on the cake. She had no memories of the event.

He stopped being her boyfriend when she was nineteen, some weeks before their first anniversary. He appeared to be honest and forthright about his reasons: he had fallen in love with another woman, a girl younger than he.

After the breakup, she found it easy to deceive herself, since she saw him just as frequently as when she was his girlfriend. It made her wonder why they had spent time so inefficiently in the days before, when he wasn't running between two women. She thought often about the lost time, or the wasted time—she didn't know what to call it.

Except she now met him in secret, away from the public eye. Taiping was about twenty minutes large (by motorbike), and the probability of H.'s (real) girlfriend catching K.'s hand in his was significant. So they rendezvoused mostly at her place, when her parents went away on business trips. On weekends, they drove to Ipoh or Penang, which, unlike Taiping, had proper malls, and there, where shoes and heels and boots squeaked on shiny smooth mall floors, he held her hand, put his arm around her waist, nuzzled her ear, and fed her from his plate.

Other than that, life seemed to go on as before. She tutored a family friend's children in the morning and left after lunch to visit him at the factory he worked in. Often she stopped on the way to get him a plastic bag of Milo, cinched shut with raffia string, a straw poking through. She sat in the empty manager's office and watched him work on the other side of the large glass rectangle. Sometimes she went over her students' homework. Sometimes she had a magazine. Most times she merely sat and followed his movements, waiting for that flash of a second when his arms strained against a handle on a mysterious machine.

After a while, K. started driving to his place on certain nights at a certain hour. The hour was his (real) girlfriend's self-imposed curfew, since she had to get up early for school. The girl was in Form Five at the Convent, long stripped of nuns after the British left. K. knew what the girl looked like. Sometimes her car would have already left H.'s yard. Other times, K. parked down the street, turned the engine off and sat in darkness, waiting to watch the girlfriend leave.

One night, by the light of a streetlamp, K. saw that his girlfriend had changed her hair, dyed it some shade of brown.

REASON: She had never left Taiping

After a year of not being H.'s girlfriend, K. was accepted into the University of Malaya. She refused to go. Her parents could not understand why she wanted so badly to throw her future away. They pressed her until she told the truth: she did not want to move away from Taiping.

"But there is nothing here," K.'s parents said. "Don't you want to leave? All your friends have moved away, anybody who can do it. Your cousins, the neighbor's kids, everybody. If you won't go to university, at least go to Kuala Lumpur, or Penang, or even Ipoh, where the jobs are better and you can make more money. Don't stay here. Here there is nothing."

She persisted, continuing to live in her parents' house. She started thinking of herself as a humble small-town girl with no ambition, no drive, a simple soul who wanted nothing more than to avoid the brutality of (real) cities, to live and die in the place in which she was born.

She would have been the first in her family to have a tertiary education.

On sweaty afternoons, when it got so hot he pushed her away on the bed, she watched the standing fan shake its head at her, a slow no no no. Often after sex he would be so comfortably stretched out, immobile, that he would not clean himself up, staining her sheets. Once, rolling off her and almost falling off the bed, he noticed a smear of period blood that K. had been unable to wash out. He asked her if she had been eating chocolate in bed. After that they always did. Cadbury milk chocolate. Sometimes with embedded nuts, sometimes not.

They had planned their first time carefully, back when they were still an official couple. Not wanting to get caught, they drove to Ipoh for a hotel room. Their first attempt was not successful; they did not time the alternating of kissing and undressing right. When he hurt her nipples, he confessed that he was a virgin, but did not ask K. if she was one, too.

After that first attempt, neither of them felt like trying again, but they had paid for the hotel room and did not want to throw good money away for nothing. To delay sex, she suggested getting food. They sat in a semi-open-air coffee shop, where he self-consciously ordered a Tiger beer. She shifted uncomfortably on the backless plastic stool with a round hole in the center of its seat. Her coffee came in a clear glass that rattled against its saucer, condensed milk lumping at the bottom.

Around dinnertime, they returned to the hotel room and managed to have (real) sex. It was the first and last time they would do it in an air-conditioned room, and sometimes, on hot afternoons in her bedroom, K. would try to bring that first time back—the atmosphere sterile from the air-conditioning fumes, stretched tight over her skin, holding her sweat and cries in. It would without a doubt be the worst sex she would have in her entire life. After it was over, H. held her very gently and apologized again and again for the pain. He had never been as tender to her since.

Driving back, they started listing places in Taiping they thought they could safely have sex in, since they could not afford a hotel room whenever they wanted to be intimate (which they imagined, at that moment, would be all the time). In the end, they were no more original than any other couple in Taiping, falling back to the reliable shrubbery in the public lake garden. The dirt and pebbles and outstretched roots of trees hurt her back at first, but she became used to it over time. Sometimes they drove to the grounds of rich men, whose properties were so large that they could not keep track of cars that parked in dark corners for half an hour at a time.

On one of the days when her parents were out of town, H. sat up on crumpled sheets and told K. that his (real) girlfriend was thinking about leaving Taiping for Johor, where a friend had connections to a lucrative job. That night, K. had a dream about the girlfriend being ejaculated from Johor, the tip of Malaysia, Asia's penis.

REASON: She was his first cousin

All they knew was that his mother had been adopted, making K. and H. first cousins by title but not by blood. K.'s father, H.'s mother's brother, would elaborate no further, either.

H.'s parents also refused to tell him how they met.

Whenever H. asked, they pretended that he was not in the room, did not exist, as if by questioning their union he himself would cease to have been conceived.

He could be from anywhere, have any kind of blood in him. K. always thought his skin color and hair type very slightly unusual. He could have been destined for another name, another race, another religion—and thus forever barred from her—but here he was! The fatefulness delighted her.

"Taiping is too fucking small," K.'s father had muttered in disgust when he learned about K. and H.

K. had very few memories of H. as a child. Everybody was happy when they broke up. Everybody was happy, too, when the cousins appeared to harbor no hard feelings and continued to be friends. It saved a lot of pain and awkwardness at family gatherings. At one such gathering, H.'s mother went so far as to whisper to K. that the other one did not measure up to her.

Sometimes, when K. and H. were bored, they would speculate about the (real) identity of his mother and how his parents had met. In one version, his mother was a prostitute who had fallen in love with his father, but shame and a sense of honor prevented H.'s father from marrying a whore. In the end the lovers begged K.'s grandfather, a client behind on his dues, to adopt H.'s mother and graft her onto a legitimate family tree.

REASON: *She was losing*

—Hair

In school, there was a girl who showed up one day with her previously armpit-length hair cut short. K.'s classmate whispered to K. that it meant the girl had lost love, probably dumped. According to the classmate, the haircut was a "symbol."

After she ceased to be a girlfriend, K. decided never to have her hair cut again. Her hair grew longer and longer and became heavier and heavier. More and more of her hair fell; her scalp could not carry the weight.

H. sometimes hurt her when he pressed his palms down onto the bed to support himself, catching her hair under his hands, yanking. He complained about the loose hair strewn over the sheets.

—Friends

The ones she lied to resented her vague excuses for being busy at odd hours of the day.

The two (real) friends she did not lie to were furious at her for letting it happen to her, "it" being at various times incest, the fate of the Other Woman, and, more generally, self-destruction.

One of the two wanted her to stand up for herself and reject the second-class, leftover scraps of love. But K. seemed unable to frame it that way. "What's wrong with small desires and asking for very little?" she asked. "It's much easier to be satisfied this way." She said she was thankful and counted her blessings that he had heart enough to not abandon her even though he had moved on to someone else.

The other friend staged an intervention of sorts and tricked K. into going on a date. The man was a well-off businessman. K. first learned about Starbucks's impending arrival in Taiping from him. He waved his hands around, telling K. about the also-impending arrivals of Sushi King and a real, honest-to-goodness cinema, something Taiping had not seen for many years. "Times are changing," he said. "Remember when that company offered to build a casino on Maxwell Hill, but the authorities refused to let them do it? Because they were afraid of spoiling nature or whatever? We missed our chance to really develop into a real city then, but look, we're doing it after all, and by ourselves, too. Soon no one will be able to call Taiping a 'small place' anymore!"

One night, half reclining on a sloping tree trunk in the lake garden, K. heard her cell phone ring. Later, when she was able to check her voice mail, she found that it was one of her two best friends, obviously drunk, calling to tell K. that she was the shame of women everywhere, allowing herself to be manipulated by a younger man so completely. "Do you know what century this is?" the friend asked. "Do you know that women have dignity?"

"I would rather have love than dignity," K. murmured to the phone. "Maybe I am just a small-town girl."

When K. got home, the first raindrops were splattering on her windshield. K. ran out of the car and rushed into the yard, yanking her family's clothes off the lines stretched out between two trees, pegs flying every which way. Her father pulled in a minute later, slamming the car door and grumbling, "Open up a Starbucks and suddenly there's a traffic jam everywhere, everybody wanting to pretend that they are city folk who can waste RM12 and three hours in line for kopi without even condensed milk in it. Taiping is just too fucking small!"

Inside the house, K. dropped the armful of damp clothes on the living room couch and called Isa, one of her two (real) friends.

"Do you want to go to Starbucks tomorrow?" K. asked.

"Oh, I'm sure it's nothing special and I won't like it, but it's something new."

KAMUNTING I

She gave herself a month. That's how long her tree of sanity would hold out in the country's most notorious prison camp, she thought, before the branches were stripped and all you could see were skeletal fingers extending upward, supplicating half-open hands cradling air, begging from the sky—please, please, please.

Isa had seen such needy trees a long time ago, in a land with fall.

Here, where she was imprisoned, the trees, even ones felled, were verdant. They spread their abundance within the fenced area in which she was allowed to roam for a few hours a day. The fences too grew things at the top, barbed wire ouroboros as far as she could see, which, under the eye-watering equatorial sun, was not very far at all.

"You lush," she said to one tree. "You lushes," she said, turning and around and around in place, a game she used to play as a child to make herself dizzy. Her dance kicked up clouds and clouds of gravelly dust, mirroring the formations above, except those she created would never make rain.

She gave herself a mouth so she could eat. She didn't have one when she was first brought here to Kamunting. She had been mute then, and so very thirsty.

The food here was not bad, really. She sometimes received whole loaves of soft bread or even sponge cake for breakfast, and for lunch there was always a sambal egg on a bed of rice.

She could never finish the food, being still carb-conscious during those first weeks. One morning, after nibbling at the two ends of her allotted loaf of bread, she put it on her cell bed, placed her head upon the softness, and went to sleep, using the bread as a pillow. The guard said nothing when he came to take away her tray.

She was the only female in the whole prison camp, she had been told. They probably meant to cow her with this fact, but instead, as far as she could tell, being a woman had guaranteed her certain amelioration of conditions. For example, she had a whole echoing prison block to herself. Even though there were many individual cells and bunks subdivided within, she was the only inmate, and on certain afternoons she could almost pretend to enjoy some power, taking naps first in one cell, then another, carrying around her bread pillow with her like a royal scepter.

When one pillow grew moldy, she simply substituted another.

Sponge cakes, despite the name, were not very pleasant at all. They did not do.

Her block was T3. It was old, with holes in the walls and craters in the floors, but at least it was all hers. The other inmates, the men, were penned in other blocks they had to share—T2A, T2B, T4, and so on. She saw some of them, sometimes, during the hours she was allowed outside her block to visit the verdant trees. The ground of her exercise area was mostly sand and stones, with gritty weeds growing sparsely in tufts, colonies keeping their distance from other clumps. Sometimes she would catch glimpses of men through two layers of fences—his and hers—playing badminton, gardening, or jogging along their perimeter, staying close to the borders.

Her second day there she was summoned to an office of sorts. The whole affair was pretty casual, no handcuffs involved. Everyone acknowledged the impossibility of escaping, what with the fences within fences and the guard-houses by the entrance. It was called an entrance and not an exit for a reason, she thought.

At the office, the man who seemed to be in charge asked her why she had brought bread along to the meeting. She shrugged.

"You're not eating enough," he said in a kindly tone. "Look at you, so skinny."

He introduced himself as Encik Vas. They engaged in some inane conversation about her living conditions: whether she was comfortable, and was there anything she would like?

"Fresh vegetables," she said.

The man nodded sympathetically and pretended to write something down.

"Now," he said. Then started questioning her about the "sodomic" poems she was accused of writing. "You're not gay," he informed her. "So why would you write something like that?"

She would say nothing.

The man tsked and shook his head.

"I still can't believe such a pretty young woman like you wrote something so filthy."

Then he let her go back to her cell. But the next day, she was escorted back to the same room with the same man, and for all she knew he was wearing the same clothes, some pastel collared shirt with dark pants, no branding visible anywhere. She saw now that they would keep sitting her down in this office, day after day, until she talked because what hurry were they in? None.

Finally, she told the man she had written the poems because she loved her country and wanted to see it right.

"See it right? What does that mean?"

"I love my country," she shrugged and repeated.

"So you show your love by making people hate it? By making people dissatisfied, unhappy, hate each other, go waste their time strolling the streets with handwritten signs instead of doing their jobs or spending time with their families?"

"I open their eyes."

"You're ungrateful. Your country has done so much for you."

"Ask not what your country can do for you," she said, almost cackling. "I did whatever I could for the sake of my country. I have no talents other than writing poetry. That is my contribution. This is my fate."

"If you say you love this country so much, why don't you respect its laws and leaders?"

"Those things and those people are not Malaysia. *I* am Malaysia. All the protestors are Malaysia. There are more small people like me than big shots like you!"

The man's face clouded. He said, "Ingrate," but she heard "inmate."

"Do you know what this place was before it became a prison camp?"

JUST HOW THE FIRE
WILL BURN

In 1936 Britannia ruled masses of land. In one corner of that empire was a leper colony. On a hand-drawn map, the colony looked to be wedged away in a tuck of area known as Bamboo River, where ramrod plants served as screens, as fences and borders. Only the strongest monsoons occasionally bent them far enough to reveal what they hid, knocking them against each other to play a harsh music.

Emaciated brown bodies shuffled or lay about the leprosarium as they were able, many assuming Bartleby's final position. The brown bodies were well taken care of by a bearded Scotsman, who had a good heart that had thus sailed him across seas for the sake of spreading basic health to the farthest reach of empire.

Not having a female companion, Dr. Berry threw himself into the not insignificant labor required for the upkeep of a leper colony. His aim was twofold: to give the lepers the best comfort possible and to shield the public at large from the horrifying disease that so claimed lives—bodies swallowed whole into it, like a suicide sucked down a dark well. It was a macabre image, and Dr. Berry did not like to think about it because he had enough self-possession to recognize that it was merely a veiled way of regretting his wife, taken from him by melancholia.

As is natural, the good doctor had a favorite inmate at the leprosarium. His name is not documented in posterity, but we can assume a few features: swollen feet tottering unsteadily; lumps for hands; neck forever craned forward and out, seeking balance that had been eaten away.

A sweet tooth caused the inmate to suck on his gums, producing hideous smacks. Occasionally, the poor soul asked "Doktor Riri" for candy from his personal stash, which was sent over by steamer along with tins of tea from time to time. To Dr. Berry, this inmate and his frequent requests for sweets presented a moral quandary. Not that the doctor believed confections would further worsen the inmate's leprosy, from a medical standpoint. But in his daily survey of the colony's inhabitants— of the bowed, spotted trees within the compound, the bamboo-lined borders beyond which one heard the hissing of a river—he was conscious that a kind of punishment had been inflicted on these men and women in his charge. And to be sure one certainly did not feed sweets to the condemned, for sweets were things signaling innocence, crafted with joy in mind.

Dr. Berry preferred to approach it as more of a monetary transaction, which was beyond morality. When he had first descended upon this strange land, he found his earlier efforts to preemptively familiarize himself with an alien landscape through field reports and ledgers sorely lacking. Navigating this entirely different atmosphere was like being forced to describe smells by using only colors; there was just enough resemblance to what he thought he knew to make him feel inadequate in the face of the untamed.

Which rendered completely forgivable his failure to immediately recognize the oddity of the currency circulating in the colony when he had first arrived, standing under the tropical sun and coughing into his silk handkerchief. Yes, the soiled paper notes and bent tin coins looked crude, bearing more than a slight resemblance to children's handiwork. But the four distinct languages crammed all over the money's surface dazzled him, harmonizing with the embarrassment of riches he saw everywhere in his new home—lush leaves and branches drooping from top-heavy trees, weeds sprouting through the dimmest cracks, fruits the various hues of plenitude. So the doctor had quite naturally assumed that the homemade feel of the colony's money was attributable to local traditions and limited native talents.

One morning, the doctor went into town to enjoy his day off. As he parted the severe screens of bamboo and gazed upon the river, he felt a shiver of boldness. What would he find on the other side? He crouched down to wash his hands in the running water, even though they were perfectly clean. He vigorously clenched and then unclenched his fists. The liquid was delicious against his bare skin. It had felt good to take his gloves off for this jaunt into the local version of civilization. What, indeed, would he find?

It was the beginning of the monsoon season then, the air just starting to be impregnated by humidity, swelling invisibly. In town, Dr. Berry walked along a pitted paved road, kicking up dust in his wake. He smiled to show he was not intimidated, even though he was the only white man he could see. Low rows of shop houses flanked him, no building over two stories high. The structures looked sturdy enough, although there was more wood and thatching than the doctor was used to seeing. The locals, unlike the buildings, did not quite look as hale as they ought to. Still smiling, the doctor peered at one or two of the men, contrasting them mentally with his patients. He took care to avert his eyes when the women openly stared.

currencies side by side, he wrote verbose observations about the differences in quality, demarcations, and design.

In vain did he ask around for the origin of the leper money—its architect, its history, its ascendance to become such common fare in this community. But the mystery remained. All he learned was that the leper money was for the good of all. It empowered the leprosarium's residents to feel ownership and claim property, while at the same time protecting the healthy from contamination. Inmates armed with the quadrilingual money traded what they had among themselves, items foraged or sent, few and far between, by relatives and friends from the outside. When one of them died, leper currency served to help divide the dead's worldly possessions with minimum scuffles. It was a fine system.

But Dr. Berry was equipped with rigorous scholarly training. He was further fueled by a need to know for certain that he would not succumb to the horrors of leprosy (a scenario that he had in truth never once considered before deciding to accept the charge of a leprosarium). The doctor now found himself within the perfect conditions for a scientific discovery. One cool evening about a fortnight after his journey into town, the doctor peeled his gloves off after a long day's work and examined himself thoroughly, gently probing flesh with flesh. Once satisfied that no symptoms had manifested, the doctor sat down on his porch to write a letter.

He smoothed crisp imported paper out on his thighs, half listening to bamboos in the evening breeze making the sounds of many polite but insistent guests knocking to be let in.

When he was done with his letter, he sealed it along with some choice leper notes, carefully wrapping them all up into a parcel addressed to a distinguished laboratory in London. And then he sat back and looked at the tropical night sky.

A slim envelope was delivered after many weeks of waiting. It contained an official report accompanied by a letter expressing keen academic interest and excitement. It seemed the doctor had caused a mild ripple among the community of his peers back home. The esteemed pillars of that community were rather impressed by Dr. Berry's unhesitating willingness to risk his own person for the advancement of science. Research using the finest instruments available in London had borne out his daring hypothesis: the quadrilingual paper bills and tin coins were conclusively proven to contain no leprosy bacteria. In other words, their particular materials were not and could not be disease carriers. It was declared impossible to contract leprosy through interactions such as commercial transactions.

What a discovery! Dr. Berry, alone in a strange world, felt a surge of grandiosity. For the first time in his life he experienced history as a force, and he wished ardently to meld himself to it. But there was no colleague near at hand to clasp, no wife to write to. The doctor looked around him. From his window he could see overgrown trees, an expanse of them, almost ringing his cottage, all rough bark and knotty skin.

That very night, the stars sleepily blinked through translucent fogs of humidity. There was barely any draft, but birds rustled leaves on behalf of breezes when it suited their avian nature. Far below, Dr. Berry strode from one end of the colony's compound to the other, rousing and coaxing.

Under his effort a crowd slowly grew, herded toward a patch of dirt and thin grass at the heart of the leprosarium. The doctor stood erect and gestured now and then with his shadow, which grew imposing, magnified by moonlight against dirt ground. With each swooping swathe of black, a leper shuffled toward the doctor, face full of defeat.

"All," the doctor said. His arm's double swung again, as if embarking on a long journey to catch up with his body.

"Semua," he repeated.

One by one, the lepers crossed in front of the doctor, surrendering what cash they had to the ground by the doctor's feet. Now and then Dr. Berry scuffed the currency against dirt to bring it closer, bit by bit molding a hill of money. The first dozen or so coins given up by leprous hands plunked dully against stones and pebbles, but as the hill grew the coins stopped protesting as they dropped, muffled by paper notes that absorbed and carried the sound deep into the packed earth.

"Semua?" the doctor asked. There was some murmuring, a movement in the shadowy crowd. Dr. Berry thought to look for his favorite patient then. He scanned faces, trying to catch as many as he could. Lesions, skin peels, discoloration, dark gaps, faces full of unmarked open graves.

He could not see the man. Dr. Berry said to himself that he would remember to make an exception and give the poor soul some candy for free tomorrow to mark the occasion.

Turning, the doctor sprinkled a fine powder over the hill of money. As the last grains dribbled away into the seams among notes and coins, he lifted his head to look at the moon. Sweat was already rolling down the side of his face. He knew that by the end of the night he would be soaked.

From the inside of his coat he drew a matchbox. He struck and it caught. With a flourish, resisting the urge to check the faces around him for reaction, he smiled grimly and tossed the burning stick onto the hill of leper money.

Without fanfare it caught fire and glowed, quickly doubling and tripling its own size, a monster of light and shadows.

The deed done, the doctor surveyed his audience once more. His favorite patient's head loomed from behind another leper's hunched shoulder. The disfigured face, with its missing bits that gave it an appearance of permanent grimace, now looked stretched with a gentle smile, contours and gaps softened by fire.

In town that night, healthy people came out of their houses and made signs for each other to look at the bright orb blinking beyond the screen of bamboos, a secret signal they could not understand. They wondered if they should.

KAMUNTING II

Over two weeks elapsed before Isa was told to expect her first visitor. Paperwork, the prison guard had explained regarding the delay.

When the day of visit came, she did her best to tidy up with the limited tools available. They had yielded to her repeated requests for a mirror, which had been accompanied by sworn avowals not to kill herself. When the hard-won victory was finally delivered, she held in her hands a child's mirror made of Plexiglas or similar, a toy with a skinny pink plastic handle.

In this mirror she discovered cheekbones.

Impossible to grant her makeup, Encik Yas's emissaries had said. She might try to kill herself by eating lipstick or eye shadow; women products all contained toxic chemicals, they solemnly informed her.

What about organic brands? she asked, almost—almost for the fun of it. She called out after their backs: "Did you know there are face creams made from fetus placenta?"

At least she had been exempt from fretting about what to wear. The clothes available to her were all soft and shapeless, including the bras—no lining. No belt. On the inside of the shirts and pants, where a manufacturer's tags usually went, were words rubber-stamped right onto the fabric:

PROPERTY OF KAMUNTING DETENTION CENTRE. She had three changes of clothes, identical.

She slowly swept the handheld mirror up and down her body, as if she were using a metal detector on herself. She wanted to know what she must look like to others these days. That was how she found four loose threads, two paint chips, and an unidentified substance that was slightly gooey ensnared in the insufficiently washed nooks and folds of her flesh.

The guards came and escorted her out of her prison block. They walked past the ugly, squat office building. Even here, where the director and his staff worked and ate, the ground was arid.

The entrance was marked with a sign saying "Visitors' Block." She made a point of glancing at the clock hanging crooked in the foyer. It was a full thirty-one minutes before the appointed visiting time. That was good. She wanted to be composed. Then again, her hair, slicked back with tap water from the bathroom, would not stay flat in place for too much longer.

They sat her down in an empty chamber divided into halves by wire mesh screens. Of course, more fencing. The halves were uneven. The side she was ushered into was smaller. There were no windows anywhere, but on the other side was a door and she stared at it, waiting, trying to empty her mind.

When she was eleven, her parents had sent her to the Buddhist equivalent of a summer camp. It was four days and three nights of prayers, mess halls, small group discussions, and sleeping on floors. Could it be—had it really been that long since she had last heard a person pray?

Eyes closed, alone but for a guard standing right behind her, she tried hard to retrieve the passages of prayer spoon-fed to them. Only two bits came: one word and a rhyming pair of phrases. Her eyes opened in dismay. She felt like a hunter who had found just a bloody paw, or a scrap of torn ear, lying limp in the traps by which she had set such store.

The one bit of word was "sarira," and it described bone fragments left over from cremation, the bits that wouldn't burn away. She simply could not remember the connection between this macabre image and the holiness of the lesson she was taught.

And the sole snippet of prayer she could recall went like this: Color is Emptiness, and Emptiness, Color. A woman with a gentle voice had decoded that phrase for the children. The word "Color" symbolized worldly possessions and concerns, as well as lust. Isa felt something shift, like a Jenga tower of memory giving way all at once when someone nudges a key piece that should have been left alone. But no more phrases or events materialized; what descended in an overpowering rush was a *feeling* that had visited her repeatedly back in her childhood. It was hard to describe, like yearning and scorn kneaded together, fingers throttling, furious mashing.

The guard behind her made a noise. It sounded like he had scraped his shoe against the featureless gray floor. Then she heard it, too, sounds of an argument from the other side of the visitors' door.

She leaned forward in her chair and strained her ears, feeling her shoulders and back stiffen. She must look like a person fighting wind, tacking against invisible force. The harder she focused on the door across the airless room, the less she registered the wire separation in the foreground, her eyes blurring out the mesh.

The medley of arguing voices separated into their components. She recognized the higher pitch as her mother, trying in her typical way of maintaining the upper hand by keeping up an unceasing torrent, as if by refusing to hear what her opponent had to say she would eventually exhaust the enemy into submission. The person she was bombarding was Encik Yas, the prison director, whose voice cut into hers now and then.

There was this nature documentary Isa had seen once, alone in the dark. It was about the ocean, and there was a scene, played out over unnecessarily dramatic music, that depicted a few huge tunas torpedoing into whirling schools of tiny silver fish. The tuna seemed to be head-butting the twister made up of thousands of the little fish, which had looked playful until the documentary revealed the end of the carnage: a whole tribe of sardines swallowed whole, eaten with their kin, nothing left but scattered scales.

She tried to rehearse how she would behave with her mother. More than anything, Isa wanted to portray a woman holding her head high under the tyranny of injustice, a poet warrior persevering in the face of dark forces. But it stabbed at her now, the idea that she could apply her free will and choose to react this way or that way, given any scenario. Color is Emptiness, and Emptiness, Color. She was in prison garb clutching her head and shifting uncomfortably on a metal folding chair. What was the point of trying to outsmart the future? Forever, always, there was only one outcome. The choice was between seeing that lone option as choosing, and not.

The door yawned, then hesitated. She could see a loose fist around the outside knob. The volume of arguing voices dialed up sharply midsentence.

". . . doing this to us?" her mother wailed.

"We will be including this in our affidavit to the court," said a third, male voice.

Encik Yas jutted his head in, jerked his chin a few times, then left, slamming the door behind him. Isa froze in terror, not knowing what the chin jerks meant. Then she realized that he must have been giving a signal to the guard behind her.

"Mei!" her mother cried out before she reached the wire mesh screen. It was a nickname she'd used when Isa was a child, a generic label that meant nothing more than "little sister." Isa had not heard anyone call her that for many years, and now she was sobbing. She felt ashamed and broken. She hadn't cried like this in front of other people, not since the rattan-cane thrashing, that awful snap of the instrument. Had she lost even her sense of pride? Would it never end, this taking away of her bit by bit? The acceptance of loss itself a loss, the broken spirit's brand of Zen.

"The director would not let us all see you at once," the stranger beside her mother said. "It's the rules, he said. One person at a time, only. But we convinced him."

She stared at him, still crying.

"My name is Surendran Subramaniam. I'm your lawyer."

"But I didn't hire you," she said stupidly.

Her mother curled the fingers of one hand through the wire mesh, looking as though she were hooking on for support. Without thinking, Isa covered those fingertips she could touch with her own palm.

Mr. Subramaniam leaned sideways and came back up with a folder of papers. His eyeballs were not white but dull yellow, made the more pronounced by swells of purplish folds creased under those eyes. His jowls were fleshy and loose, and yet he was a thin man when he stood up.

When speaking at high speed he seemed experienced

enough, briskly explaining that they didn't have much time due to visiting limitations, which was why he chose not to go through the trouble of dismissing the eavesdropping guard this time—he delivered this with a glare at the guard, whose presence Isa had forgotten.

The lawyer started discussing next steps and plans, both short- and long-term. These were the first strands of hope that had been extended to her, yet Isa's eyes kept straying and locking onto her mother's while he walked through actions and counter-actions, sounding for all the world like he was in control. She could see that her mother wanted an entirely different kind of conversation.

"Luckily you don't live far away," she said, addressing her mother when the lawyer wrapped up.

"Can't you just say you're sorry and ask for forgiveness?" her mother blurted out, her fingers' grip tightening. The screen's wire bit into Isa's finger pads. She winced.

"Can't she just say sorry?" Isa's mother turned now, appealing to the lawyer.

Before Mr. Subramaniam could answer, Isa said, "No, I have to do this. I know I can encourage other people to fight this way. We cannot give in to evil, Ma! Let them do what they want to me. For every me, there are many other people waiting to stand up for what's right! I can inspire them!"

Her voice echoed in the closed room. Mr. Subramaniam nodded solemnly, while right next to him, Isa's mother shook her head in spasmodic, violent jerks. It would have been an almost comical sight.

After a long, painful silence, her mother started telling her about a tiger that had escaped from the zoo not far from Isa's old house.

"What happened to the tiger?" Isa asked.

"They should have shot and killed it!" her mother suddenly burst out. Isa's heart beat faster; she didn't know why.

"They chased it into an abandoned taman and cornered it there," Mr. Subramaniam said.

"Which one?"

"The one with all the, uh, prostitutes at night."

"And then?"

"And then they sent some soldiers in, but they were worried they would accidentally shoot each other because of their camouflage uniforms—you know, they also got jungle stripes like a tiger?"

Isa nodded, mouth open. "Then what happened in the end? Did they catch it?"

"Yeah. They didn't have to do anything. The tiger got hungry and just walked out by itself." He even shrugged.

"Nothing to eat in the taman mah," her mother said, sounding wise. "Just like how the communists eventually walked out of the jungles all by themselves, back when I was a little girl growing up. By the time they surrender they were all skinny skeletons. You can't eat bullets, you know."

A MALAYSIAN MAN IN
MAYOR BLOOMBERG'S
SILICON ALLEY

Howie Ho knelt in front of a stacked row of dryers. The floor was cold, but the air smelled of warmth. He tried to look busy clawing clothes out of the bottom dryer. From the corner of one eye, he tracked the movement of the only other person in the dormitory's basement laundry room. The dude was rocking out to his iPod or whatever, stuffed deep into his sweater that had the college's acronym in block letters across the front.

After a few minutes, the dude shuffle-danced out of the laundry room. Howie Ho straightened up and glanced quickly around. The coast was clear. He peered curiously into the dryer above his. It was at eye level, and within it he could catch occasional, rotational glimpses of a lacy bra, playing a game with gravity, resisting it then giving in, over and over.

He had no idea her boobs were so huge. She was always wearing loose-fitting tops. Plus, she was Asian, and everybody knew most Asian girls were flat.

The next dryer over made a knocking sound. In it tumbled what looked like a giant, shaggy rug with glints of two glass eyes now and then. Howie Ho made it out to be a bear, but couldn't tell if it was Smokey or Pedo or what. That shit looked heavy. Who washed their Halloween costumes anyway? Were they planning on wearing the same one every year for the rest of their lives? Howie Ho scoffed.

Halloween had been a whole week ago, and he had been a changed man since. He had tasted absinthe for the first time. Also for the first time he had seen a real live naked girl, up close. A *white* one.

He had no idea how he'd gotten an invite for such a hip Halloween party. The theme was "subversion." Howie Ho, a computer science major, had somehow assumed it was a geeky joke, and so he'd shown up with dead tree branches and fallen twigs taped willy-nilly to his body. Nobody got the reference.

At the party, he took in the room. A gun-toting nun put down her (his?) weapon to pour a drink. In one corner were two people wearing army fatigues and ushankas emblazoned with hammers and sickles, making out.

"Excuse me." Someone pushed past him from behind, snapping one of his brittle tree parts.

Ultimately it was a very good thing indeed that Howie Ho had chosen to stay despite his discomfort. He had barely grimaced his way through his first red Solo cup before there was a commotion near the apartment entrance. He looked up in time to see a coat leave a girl's shoulders and free fall to the floor. She was naked, entirely naked. She had been walking outside in the cool autumnal air with nothing but a coat around her, and now that she was indoors, at this hip party, she revealed her subversive costume.

The room drifted cautiously toward her as if she had stronger gravitational pull than anything else. Tentative offers to get her drinks were made. Stupid, nervous jokes flew, more than one involving an orgy. Howie Ho did not move. He stood rooted, sipped his drink, and watched. After a while the girl started dancing, a loose circle of people around her. Now it seemed her gravitational pull was really a deflecting force of some kind because even though the circle was clearly dancing with her and smiling at her, no one came within four feet of her in that crowded space.

And then a Spartan, a cross-dressing Venus Williams (or her sister? It was hard to be sure) in blackface, and a stereotype of a nerd with a conspicuous pocket protector barged in, letting out a collective yelp of victory. They'd made it, hit the jackpot. The trio had been walking outside, the mostly naked Spartan gesturing wildly with his arms and roaring to ward off the evening chill. Suddenly, through an ivy-framed window, they had espied a glorious nude female form gyrating enthusiastically to loud music, which they could plainly hear because said window was on the second floor and was thrown wide open. Drawn, they leaped up the stairs, tried several doors, found one that wasn't locked, and piled in, cheering.

Here they were, advancing toward the naked girl, egging each other on, huge grins on their faces.

"Hi!" Ms. Williams fluttered her fake eyelashes.

"I'm a dweeb!" proclaimed the pocket-protector wearer.

The girl fell into helpless giggles. "That's not very subversive," she murmured with eyes closed, head lolling back, offering her throat.

The three boys gave each other looks, unsure of the ethics of sharing in such situations. Then, without warning, the Spartan extended a hand and touched the girl, his palm traveling from armpit to waist.

From then on it was chaos. Turned out the naked girl had friends milling in the drunken background, keeping watch like secret police. They swarmed in, girls in swirls of bright colors, ordering the boys to leave. Arguments and half-hearted threats to call the authorities sloshed around in the space. Through it all, the subversive nudist kept on dancing in a space increasingly tiny, her friends hemming her in.

All of the next day, as Howie Ho made his way across campus along sidewalks of trash, glitter, and vomit, he thought about the girl and refined the amazing tale, with which he later regaled every male he knew. He modestly greeted exclamations of disbelief and envy by chalking it all up to an extreme stroke of luck until Eddie, a fellow Malaysian, smirked and asked why *he* hadn't touched the skank.

"You were there, right?" Eddie laughed. "Why, no balls, is it?"

Howie Ho went upstairs to his single dorm room. He heaved his laundry bag and upended it over his twin bed. The clothes were warm. He bent to bury his face in them, then touched his erection gingerly through his jeans. The clothes smelled clean and lemony, like a girl.

The time remaining on the dryer above his had read sixteen minutes when he left. So, what, thirteen more minutes now? In thirteen minutes he would casually open his door to catch the girl next door going down for her surprisingly large and lacy bras. He would confirm for himself the size of her breasts, which he had so foolishly overlooked.

Ten more minutes. He looked at his computer. There was enough time to jerk off before the staged run-in, but then he would have to clean up and stuff.

As if on cue, he heard her moaning through the walls. He stared at the bricks, astonished. The bras! What was she doing, with her laundry so close to being done? Another high-pitched groan, this one with a tone of surprise. With annoyance, almost reluctantly, Howie Ho set to work picturing what must be happening beyond the wall.

She was Korean, he recalled. She had long swishy black hair and thighs the same width as her calves, which he found endearing. Neat, in a way. Breasts, large, yes, heaving, those neat legs soft scissors cutting his loneliness away. What? She wasn't moaning. Or she was, but not in the way he had first heard.

He squinted at his Manchester United poster on the wall. Two rows of men, one standing, one squatting. All with arms crossed. He could now hear a male voice from next door as well, clear as a bell but unintelligible because Howie Ho did not understand Korean.

It wasn't the first time this had happened. Why a beautiful girl like her with a great body would choose to tolerate an abusive asshole of a boyfriend, Howie Ho sure didn't know. The boyfriend was certainly nothing special. Last week, Howie Ho had run into him in the dorm bathrooms across the hall. Howie Ho had immediately cut his eyes away—just a regular Korean dude: hair spiked with gel, narrow eyes prolonging into fishtail wrinkles, skinny, smelling of cigarettes.

One time, she locked him out. He started off sounding calm, if stern. Soon he was yelling, ending sentences with a pound or a kick to her door, sometimes both. Howie Ho had cranked up the volume on his headphones and tried to focus on cramming for his midterm.

Now her bras were spinning prettily in a small round hole while she got shoved around again. Howie Ho never saw any marks on her when he checked her out, and Lord knows she bared enough flesh with her outfits, so how bad could it be? The dude probably pulled her hair a little, maybe spanked her ass, the kind of kinky stuff that belonged to a couple's realm, none of his business. Besides, she had voluntarily unlocked her door that time the boyfriend tried to kick it down, hadn't she? Didn't she always?

A loud crash sounded, then a thud into the wall that separated their rooms. Howie Ho's desk shuddered. There was a very high-pitched scream. Howie Ho watched as the two speaker towers on his desk swayed on their bases, rocking. He held his breath. Another scream, another thud, and one speaker toppled.

Howie Ho picked up a rapidly cooling polo shirt and started folding. He made it through that and three undershirts before padding to his door and slowly opening it, making sure it didn't squeak. All down the long, carpeted hallway he tiptoed and strained his ears, waiting for the point when the begging and crying could no longer be heard. He very gingerly pressed the button for the elevator. While he waited, he looked down at his hands.

In this dream, it was his first day in America. He was standing in the harshly lit hall of an airport, very glad to be done with the awfully long flights and the slow-crawling line at Immigration, where he had spent twenty minutes watching the girl ahead of him get in trouble with the mustachioed, uniformed officer behind bulletproof glass. His terror had mounted as he witnessed her plead, try not to cry, cry, and then be led away. She had dark skin and wore a headscarf.

Now he was out of Immigration, idling indecisively, trying to figure out the best way to get to his college. He was dragging two humongous suitcases by himself, and he had to unwrap his fists from their handles every now and then to negotiate confusing city maps. Not touching his luggage made him nervous as hell.

He walked up to a ticket machine of some sort. When it asked him which language he preferred, he was offended. What the fuck? Of course he wanted English! Were the *machines* in on it too? This whole country was participating in some kind of conspiracy, pretending they couldn't understand his perfect English.

He felt dizzy. This was a nightmare. He was pretty sure he had a great grasp of the English language, since he had to pass the SAT and the laughable TOEFL test in order to be accepted into an American college. But since his plane landed he had been unable to get anybody to understand him. He would open his mouth and form speeches that corresponded perfectly to the English language in his head, but people here either gave him confused looks and responded impatiently with *more* words spoken *even quicker*, or they would start hunching a little, and their faces would assume this sweet look of false understanding, and they would speak very slowly, and very loudly, accentuating every word.

It was beyond frustrating. He wished he were in a movie with subtitles.

The TOEFL test had featured picture after picture of two people, usually a man and a woman, frequently of different races, facing off with polite smiles. They had eighties outfits and eighties hairdos, all frizz and volume and billowy, boxy cuts. He was supposed to interpret their conversation, regular human speech broken down into multiple choice answers. For example, a woman who is lost on campus asks a man for help finding her way. The man remarks, "You're a freshman, huh?" And the woman snorts, responding with a "How'd you guess?"

Q: Why does the young woman say this: "How'd you guess?"

    A. She's uncomfortable with his curiosity.
    B. She thinks she looks older.
    C. She thinks it's obvious.
    D. She's mystified at his observation.

Howie Ho thought this was more of a psychology question than a question of English competency, really.

A man appeared out of the blue, wearing a cowboy hat and Converse sneakers that, improbably, had spurs attached to them.

"Need some help there?" the man drawled, sounding just like Matthew McConaughey. He was short, with a wayward beard and patchy sideburns but impeccably combed blond hair. Cowboy propped himself against the ticket machine like it was a set piece. When Howie Ho looked up, the sky was a dirty color.

"What's yernaime?" Cowboy asked.

"Ho . . ." he started, then caught himself. Here, in America, family names went last, after personal names. There was a joke that this was because Americans were not filial and did not respect their parents or ancestors, and that is why they put themselves before their family names. He made some mental rearrangements and said, tentatively, "Fook Hing . . . Ho."

Cowboy hooted and slapped the ticket machine on its side, creating a terrifying sound of hollowness, a metal monster screaming hunger.

Cowboy stopped, and the metal hulk hummed for a bit. Then a dime clattered into the change dispensing tray. Cowboy slinked around Howie Ho and pinched the coin.

"So, ha, Fucking Ho, what's yernaime mean?"

Behind him he could hear train doors closing, a monologue admonishing and warning.

"Prosperity . . . Rise." It wasn't easy, this negotiation of two languages.

Cowboy's mouth widened in amusement. "That's what I thought."

"What do you mean?"

"Don't worry 'bout it, buddy. Hey, there's this party. Yerwanna come?"

On the train, Fucking Ho stared dubiously at an empty seat's texture of fake grass. To him it seemed that those seats were excellent trappers of bacteria and filth, but then a woman wearing a shirt for a dress came on and sat down, squirming her almost bare buttocks into the fake grass to get comfortable. She seemed fine. He shot a hand out to steady the bigger of his suitcases as the train lurched around a corner.

"So, Malaysia is a Muslim country, right?" Cowboy asked, leaning back, arms sprawled across seat backs, every limb as loose as could be.

"Well . . ." Fucking Ho hemmed. "Kind of . . ."

"Don't worry, buddy." Cowboy laughed loudly. Fucking Ho grinned back. They seemed to be getting along well.

They walked a few blocks after they got off the train, and then they were standing in front of a house with a small flight of stairs leading up to a wooden patio. It was halfway to dusk. The air smelled cold and quiet.

The door opened and loud music billowed like fire pushing itself out of a room without really leaving it. Howie Ho stopped when he saw how packed the room was with togas, helmets, masks, and duct tape. "Whoa," Cowboy said, bumping a suitcase into the back of Fucking Ho's calves.

"You didn't tell me this was a cus-tom party," Fucking Ho said. He didn't understand why the only response he got was brays of mirth.

In the foyer were small framed pictures of children bending over the remains of a campfire, a tent in the background. Nearby, capes and coats hung like stage curtains from a coat tree, concealing some mysterious act in the dark corner. A long wig trailed from the very top of the tree.

"Buddy!" Cowboy exclaimed and waved to someone deep in the living room. He pressed a palm into Fucking Ho's back and steered forward.

"Mikey! I want you to meet this nice young man. His name is Fucking Ho!" Cowboy paused for effect. "Yee-yap! Hey Ho, here's a drink-o!" He turned around, grinned and shoved a drink into Fucking Ho's hands, then swung back and said in a stage whisper, "He's a Muslim, you know."

Fucking Ho blinked. Suddenly Cowboy's clothes had disappeared. All of it—broad-brimmed hat, heavy belt buckle, Converse with spurs. Cowboy was now stark naked, happy as a clam, or a peach, or a lark, all living things, beautiful as they breathed. Cowboy breathed too, an excited wheeze that made his chest expand and cave. Howie Ho understood in a snap that he, Ho Fook Hing a.k.a. Fucking Ho a.k.a. Prosperity Rise, was Cowboy's Halloween costume.

He glanced helplessly around the room. Discarded on the floor, presumably because they got in the way of drinking or making out, lay Viking horns, wizard staffs, juggling balls. *Tools just like me*, he thought.

He swiped a cardboard sword off the floor and hacked his way through to find a bathroom. When he found it, he pressed down on the door handle gratefully. Inside, taking up almost all the space, was a basin, tiny and round like an ornamental bird's nest. He wanted to wake up and become Howie again.

They'd met at a Southeast Asian food fair in Union Square, which, in retrospect, should have told him something. She was by herself, shuffling with neck bent to puff cooling breaths onto a Styrofoam bowl of soup noodles lifted high in two hands. Her eyes were rolled dramatically upward as she kept her sight trained ahead of her to maneuver the crowd. To Howie Ho she looked like she was worshipping the bowl of noodles. She had the whitest, shiniest eye whites he had ever seen.

"Excuse me." Wonder of wonders, *she* stopped *him*. "What's that you're having?"

He flushed and gave his crotch a single scratch, a stupid habit he didn't know he had.

"Rojak."

"What is it?"

"It's . . . Malaysian."

She laughed. It was an unusual sound, like a snort turned inside out. "And what does *that* mean?"

"Well. Let's see. The sauce is sweet, sour, salty, and spicy, combining all the flavors possible to be experienced."

"Wow!" She showed more of her eye whites. "How do you do that?"

She had fallen into step with him, still cupping her noodles. He couldn't believe it. A pretty white girl interested enough to make conversation with him.

"Uh, not sure. I only know how to eat, not cook," he

grinned and scratched. "Some people say rojak symbolizes my country. So many different races and cultures mixed together, but somehow it all tastes good. I mean, works good."

She smiled. "I don't believe you."

"Don't believe what?"

"That you're Malaysian. If you are truly Malaysian, tell me one thing only real Malaysians would ever know."

His mouth opened as he thought hard. Around them, the heat from warm bodies and cooked food seemed to echo and skid off every surface, balling their conversation up into a dull roar.

"We either think we are the best country in the world or the worst country in the world," he said at last. The pretty white girl frowned at him with her eyebrows, but her lips were curled into a smile.

Afterward, he replayed their conversation over and over, cringing whenever he came to the part where he delivered his lame answer to her question about what real Malaysians knew. What a loser! It was an opening, a wide one, and he had blown it. He could have said something like "We make the best lovers" or "We have the most charming men in the world" or *anything*, just not that earnest answer that was nevertheless nonsensical. Argh! Fucking English! Fuck the language. It was never good enough or big enough for what he had in his brain.

All in all, he was glad he had asked his boss for the day off. It was his first real job, and he definitely wanted to be in his manager's good books. But it was also Lunar New Year, and he thought he deserved the day off to embrace his roots and all, even if all he could do was wander around Union Square in the cold winter air, taking comfort from knowing he was in proximity of fellow Malaysians, who surely were attending a Southeast Asian food fair in great numbers.

And now, because of the day off, he had her number. They had spent about half an hour together at the food fair, with him doing most of the talking because she had so many questions, almost as if she were interviewing him. She wanted to know the difference between Malay and Malaysian, how many languages he spoke, whether the food she was eating was "authentic enough," the difference between Thai curries and Malaysian curries, and so on.

In contrast, he knew nothing about her, except that she was pretty and, for some inexplicable reason, in pursuit of him.

On his way home after the fair, he paused when he was halfway across the great starry hall of Grand Central. He felt lucky. He looked up at the comforting complexity of the dome, filled with line tracings done as if by an adult yearning to be a child. If someone had asked him to describe the individual depictions of zodiac figures painted on the roof, he would not have been able to recall any single one, but he had always thought of the ceiling as beautiful, and he had told people so.

He looked around him, trying to estimate how many people were there, milling or going. He picked out the younger men, on the lookout especially for T-shirts with funny sayings or bowed heads sporting practical haircuts. Anything that said "nerd."

Satisfied, he went up to a wall of ticket counters and crouched into an Asian squat, feet flat against ground. He took in the hall of people. From his back pocket, he withdrew a Nintendo 3DS. He flipped the lid open and rubbed the screen with a corner of his shirt, in case there was any dust obscuring the surface.

Howie Ho started up *Conquerors*, a game in which his objective was to build sprawling empires from the ground up. He was still at the village stage, with half a dozen mud-and-straw huts and more animals than inhabitants. He needed more villagers to build faster, so that he could get to the township level, but the game's simulated breeding and rearing process was painfully slow, requiring a good thirty minutes before any newborn inhabitant could become a useful contributor to his town.

But there was a loophole, and this was the best spot in the city to exploit that loophole. The game was decently popular, enough so that any nerdy young man walking by might be carrying another copy of it in their back pocket. This was good because the game had a "social" aspect to it. What that meant was, when two players of the game passed within ten feet or so of each other, the game granted them a villager each, fully formed and ready to build, farm, trade, procreate. Of course, there were limitations. You could obtain only one free villager per day from any given person. Grand Central, full of people scurrying across the great hall, could potentially be a huge score for him. It was a numbers game.

Within an hour, Howie Ho had added six free mature villagers to his ranks. Not bad at all. He smiled and grimaced at the same time as he stood up from his squat. He thought he would wander slowly for a bit on the other side of the hall, catch a different flow of foot traffic. His eyes glued to his screen, he started shuffling on the smooth tiles. An alert sounded: another new villager! Howie Ho glanced up, grinning, turning his head side to side. He had an urge to see who this unexpected friend and partner was.

A little boy of about six walked by—dragged, rather, by his mother, who was using her stern voice with him. "Put your little computer away!" she scolded. The little boy was holding on to his console with his free hand, spasmodically jabbing at buttons with his thumb.

Howie Ho tried to catch the boy's eye and give him a smile, then thought better of it.

The first weeks of their relationship were the sweetest periods of time Howie Ho had ever known. The white girl was a cool girl who didn't mind initiating kisses or picking restaurants. Somehow, maybe because she seemed so much out of his league that the whole thing had a tinge of daydream to it, he was not self-conscious with her. He answered her many questions without filter, questions about his parents, his country, his past life and memories. Her eye whites shone brightest when he talked, sometimes even with tears. She always wanted more details.

He bought her presents. She liked perfume in fine China bottles and books not available on Amazon. They spent Saturdays in one or another of New York's block-wide parks, listening to street performers toss music like scattered trinkets into the air.

Then, reading relationship advice online, he realized that he had not done for her what she had done for him. He had not shown that he cared by "getting to know her," a process that the advice said was really more a demonstration of attentiveness. In fact, he still knew nothing beyond the barest dating profile information—her age, her job (and how much she disliked it), etc.

So the next time they met for dinner, he made sure to hold her hand, look into her eyes, and ask her about herself.

○

Mostly she thought his life story was such a waste on him, with his bland personality. She had teased it all out of him: his grandfather had smuggled himself onto a boat departing for the South China Sea, leaving behind an entire family, generations extending back centuries, all put behind without a note.

In the new land, he met a compatriot, a Chinese woman beautiful by his standards but unlovely to the foreigners they lived among. They served each other tea and declared themselves married. And then soon after, too soon, the Japanese followed them from old country to new country like vengeful ghosts who could be neither appeased nor banished. The wife, Fook Hing's grandmother, had to shave her head to look as ugly as possible so they would not rape her.

So very many terrible things during that war. There was never enough to eat. Every day fresh tales about fetuses ripped from their mother's sliced stomachs, tossed high into the air, and then called back by gravity to be impaled on the soldiers' glinting swords, raised upward, waiting.

It was great with Fook Hing at first, but once she had mined him of his stories, his base character settled full force back in the room. Like a statue of soft clay, so full of possibilities to start, hardening day by day into a form that did not match what she had envisioned in her imagination.

She wished his stories were hers. Imagine how much she could do with that kind of material.

Once, drunk, she told Fook Hing that she wished there were no starving children in Africa, so that she wouldn't have to feel bad about feeling bad.

Reluctance padded on silent feet into their conversations. He had seemed so *authentic* when he'd first shared the details of his life and culture, but lately it seemed he was tired of remembering who he was. Fook Hing acted like he wanted more than anything to be "just" a New Yorker, living on the surface like a skim of wet on the sides of a cup, a man no more than the condensation of his current habits. "That happened a long time ago," he would say impatiently. Or: "I'm a different person now."

"Aren't you angry at your government for treating you like a second-class citizen?" she prodded.

"That's why I left," he sulked. "They can't do anything to me here."

"But aren't you still en*raged*?" she persisted.

"What do you want me to say?" He looked defiant. "You want me to pity myself, be a victim?"

He squirmed especially when she asked him to repeat stories, as if he had meant to unburden himself with the first telling. Something like an anti-Proust: he didn't so much relive memories as he relieved himself of them. By asking him to cover old ground, she was making him take back weight he thought he had dropped.

Such a goddamn unfeeling man. "Shish kebab," he had said. That was his chosen metaphor for the story about Chinese babies tossed high and then impaled on Japanese swords. She resented him for making that vulgar connection. It cheapened everything. How could she forgive him for living this way, blinkered and willing his own memories away?

She took them.

And just like that, it was over, not even enough time for the ink to dry on the business card, as Howie Ho's boss would say of any short-lived venture. Howie Ho didn't want to tell anybody about the breakup, but it couldn't really be avoided without lies because of his own damn big mouth. He had been on a different plane only such a short time ago, and he hadn't been able to refrain from bragging, just like he wasn't able to hide his dejection now.

They knew right away, his so-called friends, Malaysians one and all. There were five of them, squeezed tight around a small table that was really meant for two. This was because they had been standing in line in nippy fall air for an hour and forty-five minutes now, and they would rather be uncomfortable than miss out on such an in-demand bar. The couple at the next table was trading eye rolls of disgust over the elbows and shoe tips encroaching on their space, but who cared.

They were consultants, analysts, associates, and senior associates. Once a week they gathered to trade boasts, lamentations, and facts about all things fashionable in NYC. They prided themselves on keeping up with the world—its beat, its health, its fears, and its ids. Their livelihoods depended upon accurate readings of the global market's various moods, and they excelled at plumbing the depths of the market's multiple personalities at war with each other. History, culture, and climate were a suite of practical tools applied to corporate or national motives: this country's bonds should be shorted because its citizens had a welfare mentality (they clung too much to past glory days), and because its population was aging and sex-hating (a result of strict traditions and insular communities).

In contrast, they did not seem to do so well when it came to understanding real people. They treated Howie Ho like some sort of race hero when they found out he was dating a white girl—a *young* one.

"How did you get her to like you?" asked one analyst who earned six figures.

"Ya, what's your secret?" grinned an associate who had made a killing by betting that a certain Middle Eastern country would descend into chaos, when conventional market wisdom had it that the dictatorship was strong enough to make short work of the rebels. His lucky guess had outsmarted the market, and he was eagerly awaiting this year's Christmas bonus.

Howie Ho had shrugged modestly and chalked it all up to a "numbers game." Just try enough times, and statistically speaking, one of your attempts is bound to result in success. Don't take rejections personally, but simply practice disinterested persistence.

Now that it was all over, no one asked him for lessons learned or wisdom gained. Instead they huddled against him, trying to cheer him up in their own way. One of these ways involved pointing out hot white women in the bar and calling Howie Ho's attention to them.

"What about her?"

"Looks Eastern European."

"Ya, these Eastern European types always have such cold eyes."

"Right? I once knew a girl from—what's that place? Sounds like 'Russia' but it's not Russia."

The bar had narrow strips of mirror along the length of its wall, possibly to make the alley-like space look wider. Howie Ho caught sight of his own face. Small head, incongruously ruddy cheeks, hair spiked high to expose a protruding forehead. He looked like a triad dropout. It was a depressing thought.

"Prussia?" someone said absentmindedly.

"Is it? No, I don't think so . . . Something else."

"Belarusian? Belarus?"

"Yes! Belarus. Such ice-cold eyes, like they want you to be dead."

"I heard they are giving green cards to foreign women abused by their American boyfriends."

"Oh ya? Too bad I'm not a girl. I could punch myself a couple of times in my face and then I'm all set."

"Hahaha! That must be what they do."

When the check came Howie Ho reached for it, laughing off protests. He felt better. It was nice to have friends.

The electronic border control checkpoint at Kuala Lumpur read only Malaysian passports, as the machines had not been taught to read any other kind of embedded RFID chips.

Howie Ho approached one of these unmanned booths containing the electronic reader, eyes shiftily cutting left and right. He had experienced jamais vu the minute he had stepped out of the aircraft, humidity settling on his shoulders, making itself at home.

He had seen a Thai horror movie once in which the main character inexplicably gains a lot of weight on the scale, despite his physique changing not a bit. The climax, the twist, portrays that man coming to the realization that he has been walking around all this time carrying a vengeful female ghost on his back, perched piggyback, arms looped around his neck from behind. The ghost is upset at the man about—what was it? Howie Ho couldn't remember.

The RFID reader booth was a tiny four-by-four area marked by metal plating on the floor, a flat computer screen its only feature. Howie Ho stepped into the square. His body weight having been detected, clear plastic panels rose swooshing up from the edges of the square, flanking him at waist level.

He fumbled with his passport until it was out of its clear sleeve. The maroon document went into a metal tray sized to receive just such a thing. The machine processed, an icon whirring on screen. Then it prompted him for his fingers. Howie Ho did as it asked, lightly spreading his hand and pressing fingertips against smudgy glass.

An error message popped and beeped. Howie Ho checked his impulse to recoil and withdraw his hand. He squinted at the message. His eyes were too goddamn tired to do this, after two flights that had added up to over twenty hours. He shouldn't have binged on movie after movie. It wasn't like he could truly enjoy anything on that stupid tiny screen right in his face. Now his eyes were blurry, and he couldn't quite understand the instructions on the screen because they were in Malay, and he hadn't had occasion to use that language for years.

He checked himself again, resisting the urge to lift his face and scan the area imploringly. He knew there would be guards and immigration officers milling about. He didn't need that kind of attention. He could figure this out. But just in case they accosted him, he would tell them he was coming home to vote in the general election. Fulfilling his duty as a citizen. Surely that would put him in their good books?

Relief rushed out in a long breath when he realized that there was another line of instructions in English beneath the ones in Malay. All he had to do was press his fingertips down harder and hold them still for longer—that was all the machine wanted, to be able to take his fingerprints more accurately.

Howie Ho pressed his whole body down onto his arched right hand, the machine supporting his weight. *Take it*, he thought. *Take it quickly so I can go on.*

The machine whirred. The clear barricades went down, and Howie Ho was free to cross into Malaysia, his identity as a citizen ensured by his digits.

He sighed and walked, first dragging his feet, then picking up speed. Tired as he was, he still had to buy some American ginseng or bourbon or something from duty free, so that he could tell his parents that he had brought the items all the way back from New York.

As always, his entire family had come to pick him up at the airport, dressed in their finest clothes. His mother waved frantically at him from behind illegal taxi drivers and people holding up names on signs. His father awkwardly patted Howie Ho's spine a few times. "How was the flight? Did you eat? Are you hungry?" they asked. Every visit home had the same exact opening, fossilizing into ritual.

Except Howie Ho's sister was way louder than he remembered her to be. She primped now, the last three or four inches of her dyed hair ionized into instant-noodle curls. She had a boyfriend, and all the long drive home from the airport she reveled in describing how he was curled around her little finger.

"Yesterday we had a fight." She paused for reaction. "And he started crying. *I* wasn't even crying!" she finished triumphantly. "Clearly I wear the pants in this relationship."

They were driving past orderly rows of oil palms marking the length of a plantation. A strong wind was blowing out of earshot. The bending of trees, the ruffling of their heads of fronds, were narrated, instead, by the hiss of air-conditioning cranked high.

"Nobody needs to wear pants in a relationship," Howie Ho said. He had never been able to resist thwarting his sister, or disagreeing with her for sport.

His sister exchanged a look with his mother. Howie Ho ignored it. On both sides, trees continued streaming past, bent taut like an army of slingshots at the ready.

○

At his grandmother's house, he was surprised he couldn't recognize his grandfather, hung high over the holy altar. It was a black-and-white photo of him in his prime, whereas Howie Ho had known him only as a taciturn old man, wrung dry by life of both words and, it seemed, bodily fluids. His skin was wrinkled everywhere and yet oddly spread thin across his scarecrow body. It wasn't like other old people Howie Ho had seen. Other people's grandparents had jiggly furrows and sloughs for wrinkles, a person rattling loosely somewhere within a creased pouch. His grandfather, on the other hand, had the skinniest possible fault lines running almost under the surface, snaking in every direction, holding his frame up. Something like a kite, or those wayang kulit things, Howie Ho thought— something with a lot of skin, pulled rigid, supported by mere twigs out of sight.

They were here because his mother had insisted that he come pay his respects. He was supposed to set the tip of three joss sticks on fire, bow with them held up to his face, and stick them into the pot placed in front of a red plaque that was supposed to represent his grandfather. Howie Ho did it to make his mother happy. He had known better than to protest, even though he was tired as hell and wanted nothing more than to drive straight to his parents' home, where he would wash his feet (again, to make his mother happy) and then fall straight into the twin-size bed from his childhood.

He knew that if he had so much as murmured, she would have started in with the guilt business, berating him for failing his duties as a grandson.

"Stay so long overseas become ang moh adi lah! Too

good to be Chinese anymore, is it? Gong Gong die that time also dowwan come back, now you ashamed to see him, is it?"

Howie Ho found himself resorting to the familiar tactics of childhood: grunting and avoiding eye contact with his mother. Let her nag at him if she wanted to. He alone knew what he had done on the day of Gong Gong's death. And it wasn't so straightforward as she thought anyway. He hadn't been able to come home for the funeral because he'd had midterms. He might have lost his scholarship if he had flunked those—who knew? At the time, it had seemed an easy enough decision because, quite simply, Gong Gong could not feel his absence, being dead, and so would not miss him at the funeral.

Now, feeling his mother's eyes on his bowed back, he felt a strand of regret. A half-formed thought fluttered, then danced madly away like a fly shooed: *Maybe funerals were not for the dead.*

It'd been a dark winter afternoon, and he'd just gotten back from class. The mailbox icon was blinking on his dorm-room landline. Kicking off his shoes, he half fell onto his unmade bed and contemplated whether to listen to his messages. It could be that girl he'd left three voice mails for. But if she hadn't bothered to return his calls after a month, why would she do so now?

The blue light blinked on, and he felt hope rising within, to his annoyance. He leaned over and pressed play.

His mother sounded calm enough on the machine. She just spoke very slowly, that was all.

How many hours had it been since Gong Gong had died? And why did it always have to be like this, that delay between reality and his inner life? Every single argument Howie Ho had ever won took place only after the fact, inside his head when he was alone and eloquent. Why could he live only in retroaction, and was this what made him feel dull, not smart? Even incredibly basic things like eating and drinking—he never knew he had passed the point of satiation or drunkenness until he was hurting. But maybe, just maybe, this was a blessing because wouldn't that mean he would not recognize his own death until after his body had lost the ability to register the fact? And wouldn't this mean he would never *really* die?

Howie Ho nearly laughed but started sobbing instead, his facial muscles belatedly realizing that he was in grief and not amused. He stumbled up to call his mother back, but ended on his knees instead, almost cracking his forehead on one leg of his desk. Suddenly he was praying out loud, reciting religious texts he'd memorized in his childhood. They had never been useful to him when he'd had to learn them, and now that he had a use for them, of course he remembered only the sounds to make and not the meanings behind them. Over and over he chanted sounds he did not understand, mourning his grandfather and his inadequate memory both.

When his father called the next morning, Howie Ho apologized and explained that he had gone to bed early the night before, and so had not heard his mother's message. No, he did not think he would be able to attend the wake or the funeral. He was sorry. Yes, he was sad but doing okay.

The evening of the wake, when the rest of his family was supposed to stay up all night to watch over Gong Gong's soul, Howie Ho awoke groggily at five in the morning. He sat up in the gray light and looked at his clock. It must be almost dusk by now, halfway across the world where he wasn't.

There would be a temporary tin roof set up to shelter

guests in case it rained. Everyone in his family would be wearing white. Some of them would have patches of black fabric pinned to their left sleeves. A few of them would be crying—probably his aunt, his mother.

Because of time zones, it would be half a day in the future now, where his grandfather was laid out in his living room for all to mourn. Howie Ho wanted to follow along with the proceedings in his imagination, to participate if only in the wrong place and time. Let them denigrate him for failing his duty as the eldest grandson. He was filial and loyal in his own way. He would make it up to his family in the future. Gong Gong would know, wherever he was.

He pictured a chanting monk robed in saffron wisps of incense, then Gong Gong's face through the viewing window of a casket, powdered and colored, an alien fish seen through a porthole. There would be a framed photograph at the head of the casket, and he dwelled on the contrast between corpse and photo. But they were both strangers, neither resembling the man he had last seen. There seemed something profound in all this, and he felt it in his chest and throat. He tried not to think too hard about it.

He never told his parents about the white girl. He didn't want them to think that his sudden desire to visit home had to do with heartbreak or weakness. So he went along without protest when his mother dragged him to what was obviously a chaperoned blind date.

They were sitting under the harsh lights of a banquet hall, two youngish people and their parents spaced around a table meant for ten. The banquet hall was just a regular restaurant when no weddings were being hosted, but there were tells, such as perennial red tablecloths on round tables and deafening atmospheric noise, every ding and buzz multiplying when they echoed off the high ceilings.

The girl across from him was incredibly fresh-faced, with an even skin tone and no follicles visible, a miracle in weather as humid as this. Masses and masses of subtly dyed hair slinked around her shoulders, which he watched slacken and tighten as the girl repeatedly remembered, then forgot, to showcase good posture.

Howie Ho spun the lazy Susan in the center of the table, moving a teapot away from the girl and toward himself. The fathers were talking, but he wasn't paying attention.

"What do you think?" his mother whispered. "Not bad, right?"

Howie Ho gave his crotch a quick one-two scratch. He looked again at the girl across from him, thinking about how his skin was not at all like her skin. Even her fingers were free of the wrinkles and knobs that grew out of his hands like parasitic mushrooms. He grunted to his mother.

"Apple is studying Business Administration at TAR College." The girl's mother beamed. Her lips were lipsticked, but you could still see the creases underneath, like dry earth cracked.

"Oh, what a smart girl!" Mrs. Ho laughed for some reason.

"Aiya, not as smart as your son—making American money!" The other mother also inexplicably roared with laughter.

Howie Ho examined Apple's skinny plucked eyebrows and her button nose. He wanted to be sure she was actually pretty.

Apple caught his eye and smiled broadly. He smiled back, and it was neither awkward nor terrifying. She lifted a hand and brushed some hair off her forehead. He did not feel inadequate. Maybe it was because he already felt a sense of entitlement over her, since it was *her* family that had set up this interview of sorts.

The food came. The lazy Susan spun politely. Howie Ho watched as Apple wrapped her mouth around the top inch of chopsticks that were pinching a piece of chicken, swirled the meat around, then extracted two thin bones from between parted lips. The bones went on top of a precarious mound building up on the table in front of her, a stack of discarded shiny bones, gristle, shells, and carapace. But the latest addition was too much—the mound slid and flattened itself, spreading, revealing under it a dark stain seeping through the ruby tablecloth.

The landslide came to a stop with one prawn pereiopod resting against the rim of Apple's plate.

"Not hungry?" Apple's mother turned to him, then to Mrs. Ho. "Your son don't like Asian food?"

Howie Ho grimaced. "Jet lag," he answered.

The youngish people met without their parents a week later in a high-end shopping mall. Pavilion, it was called. Howie Ho ran his eye down an interminable line of boutique shops, counting clothes, bags, shoes, clothes, clothes, bags, female underwear, clothes, perfume, shoes, shoes, shoes.

Beside him he could sense Apple's shoulders, the part of her nearest to him. He wanted to say something, but, heck, he still didn't understand why they were here. His mother and sister had ganged up on him when he'd said he would much rather take a girl to a movie than to the mall. Trust us, they kept saying. You haven't lived here, you're not a girl. Eventually they wore him down, and he accepted their "help" as they chattered on about the merits and demerits of various malls, finally settling on Pavilion as the one with an environment most conducive to "serious dating" (as his sister termed it).

Now they were here, and he thought the whole experience rather like binge-watching bad TV. The mall's floors, waxed smooth and offering just the right amount of friction, seemed to carry his feet along as a conveyor belt would. Like a TV, the mall asked nothing of him except to take in frame after shopwindow frame of attractive things coming into view as he glided along the course set out for them. He didn't have to do anything, think anything, except: Am I bored? If so, change the channel. If not, great.

Sensing a change in the angle of Apple's shoulders, he stopped and followed her line of sight. Seemed to him that she was looking at a jean blouse with fake fur trimming at the collar and cuffs, her head cocked in a cute way to one side. The jean blouse was filled out by a headless torso bust, tightened with safety pins in the back. The hands were cut off at the wrist.

He blanched. Shocking how he'd never thought of it before, but wouldn't he be effectively halving his finances if he were to take a wife? He did some mental math, unable to avoid imaginary assaults on his paychecks staged by mortgages, loans, college funds, and jean blouses with fur trimming.

Apple was looking at him, a shy smile lifting one peak of a lip to hint at teeth and tongue. Howie Ho cleared his throat. "You like that blouse?" he asked.

Apple trilled, a delightful SMS ringtone. Then she snorted, covered her mouth in giggling embarrassment, and said, "That is the ugliest thing I have ever seen!"

Howie Ho turned, confused, to examine the blouse. It looked like a regular woman's top to him. Then he looked at Apple, still laughing, and tried to picture it on her. Yeah . . . it was atrocious.

Apple on the table, skin shiny. Howie Ho shot his sister a look of disgust, setting off waves of wide-mouthed, unfeminine laughter from her.

"I know you've been thinking of her all night . . ." she jeered. "So here's an apple for your breakfast, since you are now on the apple diet!" She laughed again, all gullet.

"You should eat it," his mother chimed in. "No time later today."

Howie Ho scooped up the fruit and ran it under sink water, ignoring his sister's claims that it had been pre-washed. He absentmindedly ran his nails around the orb, searching for a wet sticker to peel off, before remembering that his mother always bought her groceries from the wet market, where prices lived not on labels, but in the heads of the hawkers.

"I tried to buy some kuih for you because I know you like them," his mother said. "But all the stalls closed today lah, you know, prolly lining up for money in exchange for their votes. Why work when you can just get free money, right? All the protests won't change anything!"

Howie Ho loudly declared that corruption and fraud at the level she described was simply unheard of in America. He firmly believed it was a mark of patriotism to point out the flaws of his country and turn them into jokes. It was also a mark of patriotism to denounce any foreigners who highlighted Malaysia's deficiencies. Both were ways to love a country.

Right before he'd boarded the plane that would take

him here, he had felt clean, good, even moral, for coming all the way back home to cast his vote in the latest election. It was the right thing to do, as a citizen. But now everything he heard seemed to tell him that it was a meaningless act because the incumbent party was just going to win by hook *and* crook. What was one honest vote against a thousand tricks by the government?

Yesterday, a tiny polling station in a neighboring state was burned down. There were either no witnesses or no witnesses brave enough to come forward. Everyone had theories about who the perpetrators were. And by "who," everyone meant "which"—government or opposition?

It must be the government, Mr. Ho explained confidently. It was common knowledge that the government was giving out citizenships left and right to border people and other immigrants just in time for these "new Malaysians" to vote. Anybody would do, as long as they had at least one functioning hand that could palm money and scribble down votes dictated to them. With such dirty tactics, clearly the government was scared by the opposition. Polling station arson fit in with such desperation.

Mrs. Ho shook her head, sighing melodramatically. "No, no, seems more like the opposition. Angry youngsters, you know, setting things on fire because they've lost hope. They're saying, what's the point of voting? What can we do? What can anyone do?"

"But then," his sister interjected, "that Sodomy Poet caused a lot of attention, you know, young people especially, who never used to care about politics. They're all like 'free speech, free speech' now, so maybe there's still hope!"

"Is the sodomy thing really drawing the right kind of attention?" Mr. Ho seemed doubtful. "It might make conservative people support the government even more!"

"Aiya, there are more young people who want to be free . . . laws of nature mah, right?"

"What are you trying to say? Can't wait for us old people to die?"

"No lah . . ."

They set out to vote after breakfast. It seemed like an ordinary day at first, but as they neared the town center, traffic slowed to a crawl. Police milled about, standing under the shades of storefront verandas or leaning against parking meters. Something didn't feel right. Howie Ho screwed up his eyes. The buildings were the same ones he had grown up with, sides all peeling paint and dirty with whitewash from decades ago, roofs either low and flat or sloped and shingled. He had once shown a picture of this exact street to the white girl, who had remarked that it reminded her of parts of Mexico. He had been inexplicably offended. She then jumped on him, accusing him of racism, which he quite sincerely denied. Nevertheless, he could offer no coherent explanation of why he'd felt offended. How smug she was, when she argued with him.

He kept screwing and unscrewing his eyes until he figured out what was bothering him. It was the uniforms. Something different about the police outfits, maybe some embellishment or the shade of blue—*some* minor update that had been carried out between his leaving and his returning.

It probably meant nothing, he told himself.

"AHHHH!" his sister shrieked.

"What? What?"

She was holding her hands away from her, limp-wristed claws that she now pushed toward Howie Ho.

"I forgot! I got a manicure yesterday!"

Mrs. Ho expelled an "Aiya!" from the front seat.

"How much was it? Can't you just get another one after you vote?" Mr. Ho asked.

"No! It's called *indelible ink*, Ba. It's going to stay on my finger for two weeks! Maybe I shouldn't vote?"

Howie Ho surprised everyone by reaching over and gently cradling one of his sister's hands. Once, twice, he swiped his thumb along the nail of her index finger. The nail was lime green, an even, professional coating without any lumps. The polish did not spill over the boundary separating nail and skin, nor did it stay within the border. No, it perfectly *became* the border.

"This is a nice color," he said.

His sister withdrew her hand, uncertain. She blinked a few times.

Standing in line at the polling station triggered a memory, of him and the white girl walking past a clan of Asian smokers loitering in front of a bodega.

She had said, "I'm convinced smoking is a sign of regression. People want to suck on their momma's tits; that's all there is to it. The 'cool' factor was made up to disguise this infantile urge."

He turned to look at her face, to see if she was serious.

Why did such memory associations harass him? Standing in line, passing judgment on other people—the connection was the flimsiest possible. He could be thinking about a million other things instead. Why this?

He slowly pulled his wallet out and butterflied it. It took a bit of rifling before he found his Malaysian IC, nestled layers deep behind his American state ID, credit cards, and punch cards. He frowned. The wallet was too damn thick, with too many damn cards he had to carry.

He looked about. Where was the cleanliness, the moral

goodness he was supposed to feel, standing ready to perform his civic duty? Really the scene was one not of solemn ceremony but rather of agitated boredom. This particular polling station was in a boxy secondary school classroom just like the ones he had left years ago. Four long picnic-length tables formed a second, inner wall, hemming in two clear plastic boxes in the center of the room. The boxes were directly under a ceiling fan spinning so fast it was a disc of whirring. Inside the boxes were the votes, mere paper, halved or quartered, the topmost layer occasionally fluttering under the fan's mechanical draft.

They had taken away the usual rows of little wooden chairs and desks native to such classrooms. Howie Ho rubbed his thumb against his index finger, remembering the texture of those crude canals carved into desktops by pen knife blades, next to mounds of correction fluid that iced whatever surface remained. In the last year of primary school, his assigned seat had been right under a fan that looked just like this one in the polling station. He had spent many a class daydreaming about the instant gory death that would befall him when the fan detached itself from the ceiling and landed on his head like a spider with legs akimbo. It would happen one day, he knew, just like fruit inevitably ripens and leaves its tree.

There was one afternoon when something like that did nearly happen. It was monsoon season, and so it had been exceptionally windy in their fifth-floor classroom. The jalousie windows that lined two sides of the room were rotated at a forty-five-degree angle to let in air, which began to whistle as the afternoon lengthened.

The girl in front of him kept patting her ponytail every time a strong gust sang. Howie Ho watched her fluttery hands for a while. Then he slid one of his own forward, a supplicating palm held flat to receive the tips of her hair, swaying, brushing him. It tickled in a pleasant way.

His ears popped. He had no time to react. A high-pitched scream bloomed papers off every desk and shoved them sideways across the room, fighting the jealous hold of the ceiling fan, now a cyclone, struggling to beam up anything it could.

By now his classmates were also screaming, pushing themselves up and out of their seats and racing through the door, as if they, too, were being swept away by the gale. Howie Ho looked up as the fan eked out its loudest screech yet, fighting to maintain its independent, artificial revolution against Mother Nature's single-minded currents blowing through. The savage monsoon winds entered via one set of windows and sliced out another. The fan was losing, sorely and loudly. Howie Ho watched, neck craned, trying to stay still as the fan's whir became choppier. Individual blades started showing themselves through the blurry shield until, seemingly in slow motion, one single arm groaned and peeled inward, folding into itself. With each dying spin, the blade deepened into its painful sit-up, until it was finally shaped like a Come Hither finger.

Howie Ho waited for the whole thing to fall on him, but it never did. The spider spun erratically, no longer in charge.

The day before the election, his father had knocked on his door and given him a pamphlet, all awkwardness. Howie Ho flipped through it, dismissive. Just because he hadn't done it before in his life didn't mean he needed written instructions on How to Vote. How hard could it be?

He put off going to bed by watching a YouTube tutorial anyway, just in case. Thanks to it, he now knew exactly what to do, and what would happen in this crowded repurposed classroom. First, he had to go through three checkpoints before he could step into an actual voting booth. Gatekeeper number one took his IC and presumably made sure he was not pretending to be a dead person. His hand was demanded. He obediently splayed and displayed a palm, showing that his fingers were free of indelible ink.

Next, gatekeeper number two swiped his right index finger with the casualness of a government official marrying a couple. The ink, royal blue, was to prevent him from immediately returning to the back of the queue after casting a vote. If this were allowed, it was thought that a patient person could easily vote up to eight times—more if they were accomplished queue jumpers.

Lastly, gatekeeper number three handed him two pieces of paper. One was the national ballot, and the other a state ballot.

He had of course immediately scoffed at the inefficiency of such a setup, being a consultant by trade. He could pinpoint at once ten different ways of optimizing the system. Instead, he sighed. He had spent $1,500 on airfare just to cast a vote. It had felt good back in America, announcing this act of conscience to the other Malaysians staying behind for work or some such lame excuse. So now he should enjoy the moment, or commit it to memory at least. But the classroom setting was seriously killing the vibe. He couldn't call forth the somber tone and mood he thought the occasion deserved.

Howie Ho cast one last sweeping look, taking it all in: folding tables draped with fliers, pamphlets, and instructions. Lines of people snaking into each other. Headscarves and curtains stirred, now and then, under the ceiling fans.

The curtains made the voting booths look like changing rooms in old-school supermarkets, before malls had become a thing. "I wish I were as patriotic as you are," Ming had said to him, pronouncing the word *pat-trot-tic*. Howie Ho wondered whether Ming had been sincere or mocking.

Two masked men sprinted into the hall, rubber shoes skidding. One of them smacked aside a voting booth's privacy screen with a hand chop. The interrupted voter, a woman in a sari, let out a staccato of a shriek. The first man pushed her aside, then flattened himself to let the other masked man through. The second man picked up the ballot box within and hugged it to his chest.

No one was doing anything. Howie Ho cut his eyes to the person standing closest to the outside of the booth. It was a young girl with dyed hair, roots showing, her mouth agape. *Scream, girl!* he urged in his head. *Why aren't you screaming?*

The masked man hugging the ballot box eyed the neighboring voting booth. He turned to look at his accomplice. Behind them, an uncle with a thick mustache and wavy hair brought up a hand clenching a cell phone, looked at it, hesitated, then made to lunge at the masked men, the phone slightly raised as if meant as a weapon.

The masked man with hands free nudged his partner. Together, they sprinted across the room by the same route they had entered. As they charged toward the door, a woman standing near it stiffened, stood taller, then hunched smaller. Abruptly she crumpled up a ballot loose between fingers and stuffed the paper into her mouth. Her cheeks puffed. Her eyes bulged.

And they were gone. The air had the atmosphere of people shuffling out in waves after the end of a movie, but all wrong, a rude mimicry of that collective falling back into the real world after living a fantasy. Now the super charge of base reality was creating an evil vortex of sorts in the air. Howie Ho spun around, looking for his family in that choppy sea of faces: ocher, tawny, dun, sponge cake, crude oil, charred papaya. Back in America, Ming had laughingly warned Howie Ho about Nepalese and "Banglas" used to hijack the election. Scared of defeat and playing dirty, the ruling party was bussing in loads of foreigners with instant or temporary citizenship to up its votes. Howie Ho had gone online in search of proof. On blogs and strangers' Facebook walls were cell phone photos of these supposed fresh citizens getting off planes and trucks in waves, escorted by army men with long guns. He had squinted, but if he were honest with himself, he would have to admit that they looked pretty much just like Malaysians to him.

Ming said it was because Howie Ho had been away for too long. He'd lost the ability of discriminatory racial profiling that was innate to everyone born there.

Howie Ho tried to remember the features of foreigners he'd seen. All he could summon were images of guys pumping cars at petrol stations or sweaty men hanging around construction sites. He thought about a cement mixer, churning round and round. He looked at the hive of strangers around him. People were walking out, some dazed, some brisk and purposeful. He followed the stream out to find his family in the sunshine and chaos.

The restaurant built up echoes like a cave or like a Central Park tunnel, but without the cool darkness of either. They were back here again, the same space with red tablecloths, ghastly bright from cheap fluorescent lights studded everywhere overhead.

His eyes were tired. There were too many people at

dinner. Four from his family, six from Apple's. It was his first time meeting Apple's aunt and uncle. He was not ready for it, not after the clown show and the humidity they'd had today.

The aunt and uncle thought themselves witty, the complete opposite of the almost obsequious air put on by Apple's parents. Uncle and aunt must have seen the lazy Susan perched in the middle of the red tablecloth as an elevated stage built just for them, the way they went on. Already they had casually commented on the arrogance of imperialist America and the decrepitude of gun-crazy, burger-eating Americans. Now they were tag-teaming:

"Oh look, the boy still knows how to use chopsticks!"

"Oh yes! Very impressive! Maybe he should order for us. You think he can still read Chinese?"

Synchronized laughter. Mr. and Mrs. Apple were shooting the dynamic duo looks of helpless irritation. Apple herself was the picture of bleached-hair grace, making up for the lack of natural breeze in the food-hot hall by periodically flipping hair away from her face and letting it fan about her profile. She said nothing, but whenever her aunt and uncle fired off yet another cheap shot, she gave Howie Ho a sweet little smile and a look of support.

"Did you hear? This good boy here flew alllll the way back from America just to vote!" Mrs. Apple said, then immediately glanced at her wristwatch.

"Yaloh," Mrs. Ho chimed in. "He said he wanted to do his part, not like that Mrs. Lim's boy, never come home for five years . . ."

The uncle responded with a derisive baring of teeth as his wife pounced: "What! He doesn't even live here! What does he know about life in Malaysia? How can he vote? He's more American than Malaysian, so how does he know who to vote for? Just like those illegal immigrants smuggled in! Padding ballot boxes!"

"Yes loh yes loh, all he knows about Malaysia is through 'hear say.' He doesn't live here, so why should he decide who should run the place for the rest of us? Hah?" her husband continued.

"Who do you want to win?" Mr. Ho cut in. "All the young people overseas support democracy . . ."

"Ya, they 'support' by posting on Facebook and writing poems, cincai-cincai nonsense . . . Look what happened to the girl who wrote that sodomy poem for Anwar! Rotting in jail!"

Howie Ho's chopsticks clattered onto his plate. Synchronized laughter rose again. Howie Ho involuntarily turned to look at Apple. She met his eyes, encouraging smile at the ready, but it faded when she saw the fear and shock in his face.

"What's wrong?" she mouthed at him from across the table.

Howie Ho shook his head. The shake was for himself, not for Apple. No, it couldn't be. It couldn't be what he thought it was. His hand, shoved deep into his khakis' pocket and groping, vibrated like a cell phone. He was searching for one, but his pockets were empty. Then he remembered: he had been too cheap to pay for a roaming data plan from Verizon, so his phone was useless, and he had left it in his suitcase.

Fuck. He needed the internet. It alone could give him the information he needed, in a safe way. Google wouldn't demand his reasons for being curious, or probe his burning desire to find out exactly what the sodomy poem was.

Plate after plate of food jiggling on greasy trays came carried by servers. The place felt infernally hot. The others were now talking about something stupid and meaningless. At another polling station in the neighboring state, voting was over and officials were tallying up the results. They were down to the last ballot box, and it was clearly going to be a landslide victory for the opposition candidate. Even if that last box contained nothing but pro-government votes, there was no way the pendulum would be swinging back the other way. Suddenly, there was a blackout. When the lights came back on ten minutes later, two *more* ballot boxes had appeared as if by magic, consisting almost entirely of votes for the incumbent, who then managed to "win" by the slightest of margins.

The diners laughed and clucked their tongues amidst the chewing and spitting of bones. It seemed that nobody at the table believed their votes mattered or harbored any hope that the opposition would win. But they didn't seem all that outraged, cheerily swapping stories about the dirty tricks used to win elections.

Finally, the plates stopped coming, and the check was left on the table to be fought over. Howie Ho jiggled one foot after the other, mentally cursing Apple's relatives. These people were taking forever with their toothpicks, going at their teeth from all different angles, wrist motions as intricate as any Malay traditional dancer's.

And then it was over. Mr. Apple cleared his throat as he stood up. He looked first to his left, then his right, as if making sure some coast was clear. Then he bowed his neck and nodded at Howie Ho, saying, "Got time come visit ya. My wife make some almond biscuits, very good."

Howie Ho nodded back without thinking.

Back at his parents' house, he waited until everyone was settled in to watch live news of the election results on TV. Snacks were being passed around, as if they were watching an action movie. He declined. The opposition had won one key state so far. The mood in the living room was buoyant.

A commercial break came on. Howie Ho crept away to his sister's room to use her laptop. Through the closed door, he could still hear his blood relatives. He breathed out heavily and slumped in her chair. He was exhausted. In America, you stood in long lines and at the end you were given a reward, an exquisite meal or a show *Time Out* had featured. But today he had waited and waited in vain. No vote from him—and not that it mattered, apparently.

He typed in "sodomy poem malaysia." The page loaded slowly, rows of pixels at a time. Staring at the struggling page he felt physically sick, like he had the one time he'd been to a strip club. He hadn't wanted to go. It was a work thing. His boss was there. How could he say no?

"Pop his cherry!" his boss had shouted, choking with laughter, gesturing to a stripper while clapping Howie Ho on the back.

The woman smiled like she was seven and Howie Ho was Santa. She led him to a couch in a corner. When she gently pushed his chest he sat down obediently, nestling low and deep into the seat. She straddled him and began to do her thing. He blinked. Without knowing why, he found that he was watching a pole dance about fifteen feet away, sneaking peeks at snatches of the strip tease that weren't blocked by the woman on his lap.

"Are you looking at my armpit?" She suddenly laughed. It seemed like such a natural laugh. She didn't stop. He felt nauseous, his stomach churning.

Before the search results had finished displaying, he picked a couple of links at random and opened them in new tabs. One of them was just someone's blog, no ads, so that finished loading first. He scanned it. The piece seemed to be an op-ed of sorts reposted via copy and paste. *Plain and ballsy.* That was what it had to say about the poem.

He moved. His spine creaked. The whole thing made no sense to him. Why was this such a big deal? Poems were harmless, unimportant. Nobody gave a shit about them.

Vulgar. Said a different tab. *NSFW.* His heart raced again. That was what he had been waiting for, that pre-knowing deep in his guts.

A wheel stopped spinning in the last tab. He navigated to it, and there it was, the poem. *Bellies belie / anus' onus.* He read it twice, his eyes flying over the words. No. No. The white girl had written those lines; he'd seen them on a piece of paper she used as a bookmark, nestled in a book she was reading. That had been almost four months ago. He'd picked up that book and flipped through it, wanting to get inside her mind more. When he found the poem draft, he squinted at her handwriting, the strikethroughs and revisions making him more and more alarmed as he read.

At first he wondered whether she was fantasizing about exotic sex positions. He squirmed, imagining bringing the topic up with her. But the more he read, the more it sank in: it wasn't about him. He put the book down and surveyed her living room for other clues. He glanced at the closed bathroom door. The sound of water running continued from behind it.

There. On the coffee table, half-pinned by an open *New Yorker*, was a book about Anwar Ibrahim, written by an Australian lawyer. He brushed the magazine aside, revealing the book. "SODOMY II," the cover screamed. He smiled unconsciously. She must be wanting to know him better, too. That's why she was reading dry books on Malaysian politics and even composing poems about them. He marveled at his powers of influence. Imagine, an American caring about a small Southeast Asian country halfway across the world, so much so that a work of art was created!

It was morning, and the opposition had indeed lost the country, just like everyone had known it would. The country that Howie Ho had wanted to do his part in saving. The nation that had lost its bearings after being bounced around multiple colonial masters like an ugly ornament that kept on being regifted.

"I'm sorry you flew all the way back for nothing," Mr. Ho said. Then he changed the subject, complaining about his left eyelid that wouldn't stop twitching.

"That signals disaster," Howie Ho's sister said helpfully. "If it's right eyelid that's okay, that means you get rich."

Mrs. Ho was dejected. She had gone to bed when initial numbers pointed to an opposition victory, dreaming of a new dawn. Now she blamed herself for the overnight robbery, which, it seemed to her, wouldn't have happened if she had kept vigil.

A mosquito attached itself to a spot just below Howie Ho's elbow. Its crawling legs blended in perfectly with the hairs on his arm. He froze. He couldn't think. Isa Sin, the real one, the scapegoat rotting in jail—he had looked up a picture of her after reading the sodomy poems. It had been a whole month. They must have kicked her ribs in by now, made her tiny bosom concave. And then they must have starved her before splashing boiling-hot broth all over her, laughing while she bit down her screams and licked her own burning arms for scraps of soup, red red red.

"Ahhh!" he yelled. His sister had brought an open

palm vigorously down on his forearm. The clap was like thunder. Ears ringing, he shoved her hand away. There was a little smear of blood and hair-thin legs splaying out of the blob.

"What's wrong?" his mother asked.

"I feel bad," he muttered.

He went back to his room, waving off her concerned tittering. Good thing the landline in there still worked. He drew his chair close to the desk and called his airline. He cleared his throat and scratched himself as the phone rang.

"Hello?" he whispered when the dial tone stopped. Best if his family didn't hear him. He wanted to leave, right away—he couldn't stay here anymore.

But it couldn't be done. All the flights to America were already booked over capacity. He would have to keep the return date on his current ticket. He hung up, fearful.

"Where are you going?" Mr. Ho asked when Howie Ho hurried past the kitchen.

"Going out!" He didn't stop. "For fresh air," he added.

"There's no such thing in this place!" Mr. Ho shouted after him.

Nobody could call him selfish for trying to be a good son. A good son was someone who married a nice Malaysian girl and made nice Malaysian babies. Today was the day; it was now or never; time waits for no man; etc. His parents had always nagged him about being a good Asian man who respected his roots and continued important traditions like filial piety. "The tree wants to be still, but the wind will not cease," his mother often cajoled in her backhanded way. The rest of the proverb went, "A son wants to take care of his parents, but they are no longer present."

He felt as he did before big meetings at work, when the

PowerPoint presentations were as polished as they would ever be and he was sitting in an empty meeting room, having arrived ten minutes earlier than everyone else. He was ready. Nothing could go wrong as long as he was prepared. And he always was.

He had crunched the numbers three times and each time the satisfactory answer was that, yes, he could indeed well afford to get married, thus fulfilling his parents' fondest wish. Thanks to the prudent financial decisions of his early twenties, he was now able to comfortably take on a mortgage and a wife who spent moderately (no more than two overseas trips per year).

The only wrinkle so far was that he had left the house later than expected, all because Mrs. Ho had taken issue with his choice of clothing. Unfit for such an important occasion, she had lectured. He protested that Malaysian weather was much too hot and humid for something like a Western suit, but his mother vehemently insisted that he not bring shame to the family, an admonishment that always worked in the end.

Howie Ho crouched into his father's car. A jet of air-conditioning hit him squarely in the neck. He shuddered. For no reason, he turned to look at the empty back seat. Somehow Gong Gong seemed to be with him. Maybe Howie Ho would be forgiven now, on his way to be a good son, one who married a nice Malaysian girl and settled down within driving distance of his parents so that he could play mahjong with them once a week. Through this he would be redeemed.

It was indeed blazingly hot. He pulled to a stop at a traffic light and stared at the windshields of cars on the opposite side, shimmering, opaque, looking one moment hard as diamonds and the next on the verge of melting. His brain felt like that: blank and yet not quite blank, alternating between invincibility and vulnerability.

The light changed. The car behind him honked, startling him into making a rash wrong turn. He braked almost immediately when he realized his mistake. The other car screeched and honked even louder. He stalled on the shoulder of the road, barely looking up when the other driver pulled past with an open palm jabbed energetically toward Howie Ho.

He was nauseous from the sun. *Funny how your body evolves so quickly,* he thought confusedly. *My cells must no longer be accustomed to this brutal weather.* He put his head down on the steering wheel to stop himself from imagining the individual shriveling of each capillary.

Think positive, he exhorted. Yes, think about how cheap it would be to move away from America, and how legitimate an excuse. He was exhibiting behaviors of a good member of society, seriously pondering settling down and raising fine children. America's metropolitan cities are no place for that kind of adult activity, after all. If he had a wife in tow, no one could say he left because he couldn't cut it in the Big Apple, right?

Another car honked from behind him. He ignored it. The car honked again. His face immobile against the steering wheel, he raised a hand above his head and pawed at the air, waving the car forward. Finally, he heard it rev and advance. But then it seemed to slow and pull up parallel to his car, idling there next to him.

Shit, what a bother. They probably thought he was having a heart attack or something. He was about to raise his face when there was thunderous rapping against the glass pane, right in his ear. He jumped, heart jackhammering. The face looming was his sister's. She looked almost like their mother when she was worried. Behind her, haloing her head, were tree branches gently shaking out their leaves in a gust of breeze.

She moved her mouth but he couldn't hear her. Hands shivering, he cranked down his window.

"You forgot your flowers," she smiled, holding up a bouquet, one of the nicer ones that came with multiple layers of wrapping. They smelled like a department store, he thought.

"I din buy flowers," Howie Ho murmured. Roses, of course, rich and unreal in this tropical weather.

"Oh . . . Maybe you forgot? They were on the kitchen table. Almost got curry on them . . ."

Howie Ho peered up at her, framed by illuminated leaves. She shifted the flowers from one hand to the other. Sweat was starting to form on her brow. He took the flowers from her, navigating the bunch awkwardly through the car window. With every move, the inner layer of clear plastic wrapping rasped against the outer layer of pastel paper that had scalloped edges. When he dropped them onto the passenger seat they made a noisy shuffle.

He turned to thank his sister and saw that she was already getting into her car. "Thank you," he half shouted. She met his gaze and smiled, then pulled ahead and drove off.

The Apples' double swinging gates gaped wide when Howie Ho pulled up, already late. He cut off a song mid-chorus on the car radio.

The house of his future in-laws was unremarkable, a unit in a row of identical single-story homes. The sameness of the houses seemed to have a side effect of spurring on various spurts of creativity and self-expression. Retirees, housewives, and other homebound owners grew very passionate about gardening, vying to color their front yards with the gaudiest flowers. That, or they decked out their houses with cultural icons and kept assorted decorations swinging in the wind long after their associated holidays had passed. Anything to make their cookie-cutter units stand out from the rest.

The Apples' tiled roof, once a bright blue, supported an Astro satellite dish. A gutter lined the roof's rim, collecting rainwater and brown leaves. At the foot of a cement driveway were the front gates, and just inside the gates' prison bars lay a garden hose, curled up on itself like a domestic animal.

He slammed the car door shut, then saw the roses still in the car, almost sagging off the seat. He opened the door again. The flowers now smelled acrid sour. He fondled a petal. The texture somehow reminded him of sashimi, of all things. There was a word for it, wasn't there? What was it?

Papa and Mama Apple were sitting prim-legged on a loveseat facing the front door. They accepted his flowers and his apologies for being late with flinty cheeriness. Apple was nowhere to be seen. Howie Ho imagined her lurking in the next room, occasionally peeking around the corner, hair waterfalling over her pretty face.

Outside, a truck rumbled by, crunching the tar road. Mrs. Apple disappeared with the flowers and returned with tea, biscuits, and a wide grin. She left again almost immediately, to check on her daughter, or so she said.

"So, young man." Mr. Apple cleared his throat. "You interested in my daughter, huh? Well first you have to answer some questions. Number one, how many girlfriends you have?"

"Haha . . . Uncle," Howie Ho laughed weakly, deciding

to start with a safe honorific. "No girlfriends at all, I am a straightforward and loyal man."

"Mm. Good. How about in the past? How many before this?"

"Don't worry, Uncle. I'm not a playboy."

"So many you can't remember?" Mr. Apple twisted his mouth sideways, indicating a joke.

Howie Ho laughed politely again. He felt he was laughing too much and that it somehow put him in a weak position, but what was he supposed to do?

"Not many, maybe two or three only."

"What about ang moh? You dated American girls before?"

He swallowed. "Only one, Uncle. It wasn't serious."

"Hmm," Mr. Apple looked thoughtful. Here Mrs. Apple mercifully returned, not with Apple but with a giant bottle of Fanta. She set it down on the coffee table's glass top, and the Fanta immediately started wetting itself, pooling at its base.

Mrs. Apple coughed. "The flowers are very sweet," she said, and for a confused moment Howie Ho wondered why in the world she had eaten them.

Sometimes it takes an outsider, someone with distance and perspective, to cut to the heart of the matter, especially for such complicated subject matters enmeshed in ethnic enmity.

I don't want to listen to you right now, Howie Ho thought sternly to the white girl in his head.

In the corner of the Apples' living room was a dust-sheeted piano, an empty, dry fish tank balanced on top.

You told me yourself that you trust only foreign news about Malaysia, the white girl continued. *Because of censorship, remember?*

Howie Ho tried to summon the good feelings he should be having. That first-day-of-the-year, first-visit-back-to-the-gym-after-a-long-hiatus aura of purposefulness, recharged energy, and courage—*that's* what should be enveloping him at the moment, one of the biggest in his entire life.

He began formally, "Uncle, Auntie, I came here today to let you know that I want to—hope to—propose to Apple. I hope you will give your blessing . . . ?"

Mrs. Apple's eyebrows wagged from side to side. She smirked happily. Mr. Apple, on the other hand, assumed a serious expression.

"Will you take good care of my daughter?" he asked.

"Yes, of course. Otherwise, Uncle, you will beat me up, right?"

From somewhere deep in the house came the accelerating echoes of a metal object dropped and spinning itself in circles until spent. Apple, with a tray? Did he say something wrong?

"US very good, right? Not like here, everything corruption, police cincai jail people," Mr. Apple said, smiling broadly as if he were imparting good news.

"You want to buy house, or you think condo is better investment? I heard real estate there is big, big opportunity!" Mrs. Apple cut in.

Something was off. He knew it, but he could do nothing except push forward, follow his script.

"I saw a house the other day—I mean, just a computer model, but looks nice, two stories, got balcony some more, very grand." He remembered to look each parent in the eye in turn; that was good. "It's a prime location, not far from Cyberjaya—"

"You mean you're not going to live in US?" Mr. Apple interrupted, stressing syllables. It sounded like he'd said *you ass*, and his frown lines were somehow deeper, liver spots darker.

The house wasn't in the United States, Howie Ho

explained. He didn't feel right uprooting Apple and taking her so far away from her family; it was time for him to settle down and what better place than home; he was ready; born a Malaysian, always a Malaysian, ha ha. Momentum kept him going through Mrs. Apple's rapidly evolving facial contortions, going from surprise to dismay to, finally, anger.

He petered out. The house was quiet. Howie Ho thought about the white girl, free as a bird, and about Isabella Sin, a stranger to him—jailbird. He knew he had fucked up. He would not be getting married because he was auditioning for the wrong role. As they walked him out, he craned his neck to see if Apple might be watching from somewhere in the back of the house. He saw only cool teal walls and understood that he was nothing without his American identity, borrowed.

Back home his family rallied around him, exclaiming, maligning the Apples. What blind idiots, as if marrying a wonderful, *highly* educated young man like Howie Ho were not the luckiest thing that would ever happen to her! They think the moon is brighter in the West! Watch, if you had married her and moved with her to America she would have divorced you for a white guy as soon as you landed. I know her type! Did you see how blond her hair was? Fake to the max.

Howie Ho, exhausted, begged them to stop. In the sudden silence, Mrs. Ho timidly said, "I din know you wanted to move back here. I thought . . . you had become American."

Her voice was tender. She looked at Howie Ho. He shook his head mechanically, kept shaking until her eyes dropped.

That very night he started packing his suitcases, even though his flight was not for a few days.

"Ma asked me to give you this." He jumped at his sister's voice. She was holding out a packet of ginseng tea. He took it and turned it over in his hands, ignoring his sister's stare. He knew that she knew he would not finish the tea before its expiration date, and that the next time he came back to this house it would be for a funeral.

She sat down on his bed, next to a tower of sloppily folded clothes.

"You know, I used to hate you."

Howie Ho grimaced, thinking of the time he had punched her for real in the stomach. They had been fighting over a toy he couldn't even remember.

"I'm sorry. I guess I wasn't very nice."

"No, no. You were a good big brother. It wasn't your fault. But you know why I hated you? You remember the cane on top of the bookshelf?"

She paused and peered keenly at him. Yes, he remembered. He had scraped up a chair and fumbled at the top of the bookshelf when everyone was out, disturbing dust, convinced he would find porn magazines in such a good hiding place. He remembered the cane, cool to the touch. Rattan or bamboo it felt like, disarmingly light in his hands.

"Ma beat me with that cane. Well, not that one—she had to buy new one each time after caning me. Ba made me lift up my skirt so he could cane me on my backside. They punished me together, two of them."

She was looking at him, wanting something. But what?

"They never touched you. You did worse things and they never beat you. Why? Because you're a son?"

Howie Ho said nothing. What did she expect him to do?

It wasn't his damn fault, like she said. Wasn't his problem to fix. He couldn't do anything about it.

"They saved money to send you overseas, but what about me?"

She stood up too quickly, making the bed's surface bounce. The leaning tower of folded clothes toppled, slow and silent, until it fanned itself out into an arc.

There were video games that he played in which, if he died at a monster's hand (or claw or fang), he (or rather, his character) would respawn and he would have to face the same monster, again and again, until he beat it.

That was what this airport scene felt like, each and every time he left home, down to his very same misguided optimism that every repetition would be the last—this time he would finally whup it. Except he wasn't quite sure what the monster he needed to slay was. All he knew was that he was tired of his mother's wailing and public scenes, and also of the sickening drop in his stomach whenever an immigration officer frowned.

Ten years ago, when he had first left for college in America, Mrs. Ho had clung on to him in a desperate hug and sobbed repeatedly, "He'll never come back!" She cried into his shoulder, talking to him about himself in the third person. "I lost a son today! He won't want to come back anymore, I know it!"

How he had protested then, indignant that she could assume such a thing about him. What did she know about him? Not his heart! Not his soul.

Ten years later it was still the same refrain. It hardly even made sense anymore; everyone knew he was well settled into his life in another country. She was probably just doing it to guilt him, in her usual passive-aggressive way.

"Time flies," Mr. Ho said, standing awkwardly to one side. The airport's bright lights accentuated the thinness of his hair, but they also made the strands shine silver. One thing you could count on from him was trite sayings, delivered especially frequently in the face of Mrs. Ho's public displays of emotions.

"Do you miss home?" Americans would sometimes ask Howie Ho. After years of the same question he had a standard answer, offered up automatically and without thought. "I miss the food," he would say. And they would always nod in understanding. He never questioned what it was they were agreeing with.

The airport was full of beeps and clicks, an unceasing background noise that made him feel like he was trapped inside a giant machine. And he was, wasn't he?

Finally, it was time to go. Mrs. Ho wiped her eyes and waylaid a stranger to help take a cell phone photo of the family. "Who knows, this might be the last one," she said, serving up a loving parting jab as she put the weight of her arms around Howie Ho's neck.

And then he was walking past security guards who protected him from his family. The guards wagged their uniformed necks and droned, "Boarding pass only, boarding pass only."

"Bye!" he said.

"Bye!" "Bye!" "Bye!" they said.

He crossed the wide hall to the immigration checkpoint. Turning back for one final look, he saw his family waving silently, each of them with one hand up and the other fisted, moored to the railing in front of them.

He emerged into the international terminal of the airport. The first thing he registered was a lady with pasty skin getting a pedicure right there in the open, sitting hunched in a massage chair that was tilted all the way back. A very young woman was serving her, wearing a mask, a cap, and an apron, scrubbing dead skin off feet. The next stall over was a bakery, its enticing smells mingling with nail polish to produce a truly foul odor.

His eyes glazed over as he took in the signs of each store-front, pushing his baggage slowly along. His plan was to treat the airport like a shopping mall and kill time until he had to board. He looked at his watch, converting the time to Eastern. Already he could feel his shoulders relaxing. Being in transit was always one of his favorite things. It was when he felt absolutely no guilt over eating McDonald's or watching six blockbuster action movies in a row. Nothing counted when you were in transit—it wasn't really you, gorging on junk. You were on vacation from yourself.

A man in a shirt and tie strode past, trailed by a sol-dier cradling a machine gun. The man's plain white shirt was crumpled in the back and tufting from his waistband. Howie Ho tried to take a closer look at the gun, which looked longer than his arm. He blinked and the man had turned around, meeting his eye. He paled. Man and soldier were beelining for him. He slipped his hand into his trouser pockets and felt for the reassuring edges of his passport. He ran his finger flesh along the rim in nervous strokes.

"Sir," the man said. Nipples showed faintly through the front of his shirt. The soldier stopped a few feet behind the man. The machine gun had a sling that the soldier wore in textbook anti-street-theft style, cross-body, the same way Mrs. Ho carried her handbag when she felt she was walk-ing through unsafe neighborhoods.

"Passport, please," the man said. Howie Ho snapped to, fumbling with his pocket. "Just a routine inspection, sir," the man continued.

He bent his head to examine Howie Ho's maroon passport. Howie Ho could see the clearly demarcated lanes of the man's gelled hair, lines perfectly parallel, as if the man were in the habit of using his crown as a Zen garden.

"Hmm," the man breathed, flipping a page. Howie Ho's heart was dive-bombing against his rib cage. No, it couldn't be *that*. Isa Sin? Could it be? He had done nothing wrong. But was that why? He would be punished. They would not let him go to America now, not now, not after—or was it before?—what he—didn't?—do.

His hand rose weakly to press down the pain in his chest. The soldier tracked the movement from the corner of his eye. He had a head-on view of Howie Ho, but somehow managed to convey a slit-eyed, sideways look.

The man with the tie wiggled Howie Ho's boarding pass out of the passport. *I don't know her*, Howie Ho wanted to announce in a calm and dignified voice. He stopped breathing, waiting with dread for the man to slowly tear the boarding pass into halves, quarters, confetti. Instead the man took out a pen and uncapped it. With a flourish, he made a mysterious marking on the boarding pass, a rune, sharp angles alternating with round corners, a severe line cutting through the whole.

Howie Ho looked at the man's face, waiting for something to be revealed, but the man was already handing the most important thing in his life back to him, and Howie Ho breathed out to realize his ears were ringing.

Later, seat belt snug against body in his assigned seat, Howie Ho caressed the screen of his cell phone, fingerprinting it again and again. Soon a stewardess would come by and admonish everyone to turn off their electronics, and then it would be too late to send his family one last message of love or something. He fondled the phone's little micro-USB slot and headphone jack until the admonishment did come. Then he put the device away and closed his eyes. He tried to call up details of his father, mother, and sister's faces, the back of his head shoved into the headrest like he wanted to prevent memory from leaking out.

Oh, but he wanted to do the right thing, he really did. Of course he felt bad about an innocent woman locked up for poetic crimes she didn't commit. But he wasn't the perpetrator. Why should it fall on him to do something?

Slowly, he realized that he had of course been massively relieved earlier, yes, when they'd handed back his passport, but he had also been disappointed. It was the same feeling that had cocooned him when the Apples had rejected him. He knew the right answer, and he did want to make everyone happy. If only the man had confiscated his passport—*then* he could do his duty—then he could be good.

BRIGHT AND CLEAR

Mother asked the question I had been dreading all morning, when she finally admitted that we were lost.

She started with a sigh. "Lost again. I just have such a terrible sense of direction. So, you still a lesbian?"

"Unfortunately, I am still seeing Meena," I said, stressing words where appropriate. "I can't just change who I am, you know, much as I'd love to."

"Oh really? You used to date boys in secondary school. Now you date girls. So, if you can change one way, you can change the other way, right?"

"Maybe we should stop," I said, not wanting to meander farther down unfamiliar little mud roads. But my mother misunderstood. Her lips clamped, and her butt shifted on the driver's seat. The car moved on. Pebbles sent flying by rubber wheels hit the underside of the old Proton Saga and clanked gratingly.

Mother, tapping the steering wheel, told me to help her find our way. Annoyed that she had been predictable enough to ask what I'd dreaded her asking, I said, "If Dad were here we wouldn't be lost."

"Well, we're going to see *my* parents, not his," she replied.

"*He* always drove before," I shot back, and was immediately unsure of my point.

Outside the car was an army of orderly rubber trees, each ringed by neat diagonal wounds that bled dirty white, like the eraser in my pencil box from when I first learned to write.

"You think those are the same trees we passed earlier?" Mother asked.

"I think we should ask that woman for directions."

Mother looked at the advancing figures and shook her head. "She's Malay."

"So?"

"So? Why should she know where a Chinese cemetery is lah?"

"If we were in our taman and this woman asked you where the nearest masjid is, wouldn't you be able to answer her?"

Mother slowed the car. The woman paid no attention, but her goat looked at us briefly. I cranked down my window. Squeaky.

"Kak, can you tell us where the Chinese cemetery is?"

She looked up, her face impassive. She lifted a finger, twisted her body, and pointed. Then, wordlessly, she adjusted her tudung and prepared to leave.

"Nice goat," I said.

"Goat? What?" Her eyeballs pushed out. "Not mine lah. Why would I have a goat?"

We wound our way up hilly slopes and weaved through rows and rows of gravestones, some more erect than others. The sun scorched us. Mother carried the fruits, incense, and cold roast pork. I carried large bags of folded paper money, fingers massaging the lighter in my pocket.

Mother walked in front and got us lost among the tombstones. She sweated and swiveled her head about, trying to find my grandparents.

"Ow!" She stubbed her toe on someone else's gravestone. A Mr. Szeto's.

"Sorry," she mumbled to the dirt ground. She turned around to look at me sadly. "You're right. If your father were here we wouldn't be lost."

Her concession made me feel so guilty I almost believed that she had said it to play victim. But her bowed back reminded me that I had been rude to her when she had called me almost every night when I was in London. She had wanted to talk about the divorce and her menopause, but I'd had no patience for her then. I did not want to be reminded of being a woman.

I took a couple of quick steps and held her elbow. "I see them, over there."

Like every year before this, I silently rememorized my grandparents' given names and swore never to forget them. Grandfather's name was much more vivid than Grandmother's; the paint had not had as much time to chip away.

We went through the motions, and it was hard to tell how upset I felt, traditions being the great neutralizer of emotions in my case. Around us, the hill swayed and slid with the combined weight of all its graves. Mini pyres burned elsewhere, lit by other families. Each family followed its own customs: some ate fruits meant for the ghosts lingering about, while others warned against touching any food. Grass tried to grow everywhere and over and under everyone.

The swimming fire and smoke finally made my eyes water. Lifting my arm, I beckoned Mother to join me where I sat on the neighboring gravestone.

I told her about that day when I was all alone in our old house. Rain hammered on the zinc roof of our neighbor's chicken coop, and the racket somehow made me conscious that I was bored. I started rifling through my father's filing cabinet. "You know, the one he keeps our tax stuff in"—I looked at Mother. She shook her head, and my disdain rose again. How clueless she had been, about her own life.

There had been reams of mortgage documents, electricity bills, bank statements, train schedules—such things. And underneath them all, wedged against a back corner, was a black plastic bag with handles. Inside I'd found about a dozen VCDs. Their covers showed me what my father desired sexually, and when I came across the schoolgirls in uniform I had to think about my blue pinafores. How could I have not?

I told my mother how I sat down in front of our TV and watched most of Dad's collection. I told her that I'd found myself turned on, and when I got up to go to the bathroom I'd looked down to see moist patches.

It was a horrible story. I didn't deliver the punch line, but it was there, evident and blatantly false: I was queer because of Dad. I watched Mother's face. I wasn't sure what I wanted to see. Only later in life would I learn to regard my preference of anger over sadness as problematic. Right then, surrounded by graves, all I wanted was for my mother to hate my father.

Mother got up and went back to the grave we were visiting. She closed her eyes and started whispering to her parents, and suddenly I was terrified. What would I do when it was my turn? I was ignorant of the ceremonial steps performed in cemeteries.

On our way back we got lost again. For the fourth or fifth time, we passed the rows of rubber trees, more orderly than graves and human lives. I didn't stop Mother when she started telling me all about Taiping, as if I were a tourist.

How it almost became the capital of Malaysia before the honor went to a nowhere place at the cross-streams of two dirty rivers. How Taiping had fallen from glory, its claim to fame sad relics of a colonial past. How that confused its dwellers, made them unsure of how to gossip, how to be friendly, what kind of food to like, whether to be full of hope or devoid of it.

A car pulled up next to us, and its driver asked if we knew how to get to the clock tower, "the oldest one in the country." Mother, suddenly cheerful, said, "You're going the wrong way. Gostan, gostan!"

TAIPING

Dawn at the foot of Maxwell Hill was chilly enough to conjure memories of Cameron Highlands, where they grew strawberries and roses and other such improbable Western things. Now *that* was a hill that had truly been elevated to a proper tourist attraction. The Cameron Highlands had a dedicated website that looked pretty good. On the website, you could look up tour companies and choose among hotels ranging from two to five stars. Maxwell Hill had no web presence, only one accessible road, and an abundance of mosquitoes to greet visitors. Here, the choice for tourists was whether to leave windows shut in rental houses without air-conditioning or to open the windows and collect insect bites as souvenirs.

The retired assistant branch manager, being a believer in the afterlife, wondered how the dead white men respectively felt. Sir William Cameron went on his native adventure and discovered his highlands on elephant back. In contrast, Sir (William) George Maxwell arrived, took up his colonial post, and just like that, got a hill named after him by sitting behind a desk.

Sir Cameron must be declared the victor, thought the retired assistant branch manager. After all, no one was proposing to erase the marks of colonization from Cameron

Highlands. Whereas Maxwell Hill had been rebranded Bukit Larut, a name that made the uninitiated think of boulders, trees, grass, and mud melting into a hilly puddle. Funny that it was Sir Maxwell who first proposed turning Sir Cameron's highlands into a resort, starting years of construction that ended in carefully manicured rose gardens, pesticide-sprayed strawberry farms, and hotels that printed long lists under a section named "amenities"—ordinary household things like hairdryers and electric kettles. As of the twenty-first century, the Highlands were a hub of foreign tourism, while Maxwell Hill shimmered like a mirage of a ghost town behind its latest name.

Although to be frank, if you'd asked the retired assistant branch manager, he would have said Maxwell Hill was the true winner. He'd always said he preferred unspoiled natural beauty to commercialized family fun. A simple man, he called himself.

Perhaps that was why he felt such affinity for this town, when he should have perhaps resented it. It was a place he had not seen until well into adulthood, when he started taking a bus down to court the woman who would become his wife, bear him a child, and then leave him in his twilight years. Taiping was the site of old dreams: unburied, unforgotten, in your face daily under the prickly heat of the tropical sun. Almost became the country's capital, it did—until an upstart fishing village situated between the two warm thighs of Gombak and Klang rivers snatched the title right from under Taiping's nose.

And what was Taiping to do, except make the most of it? It preserved its claim to fame by continuing to lock animals and people up in the country's oldest zoo and the country's oldest prison, respectively; by erecting a plaque commemorating the country's first railway station; by letting the sun polish colonial planes, cars, cannons, and statues in the courtyard of the country's oldest museum. All this so that bored teachers could chaperone sweaty kids in school uniforms on weekday visits to the town, coming with discounted group tickets and leaving behind Rota snack wrappers. Meanwhile, parents eager to take glamorous vacation photos with their kids drove to cool places like the Cameron and Genting Highlands, sites of elegance and opportunity, not of decayed glory. Where they could pose in their sweaters, windbreakers, and jackets. Paying money for the luxury of experiencing Cold, which was representative of something else.

Other places developed. Taiping preserved. Here, he was surrounded by objects standing in for his wife's presence, like how hills stood on all sides of the teardrop-shaped town, not in an embrace, but the way you would cup a palmful of water in order to trap a twisting fish.

Lately, he had been trying to make a list of reasons why he loved Taiping. He wasn't trying to convince himself—he knew, in his bones, that the way he felt was true. But other people required articulation, particularly when they asked him how things were going between him and his wife, or why he was staying on in that empty house all by himself. It was just like on their wedding day, when he'd known in his gut that he wanted to marry her, but other people had wanted him to list his reasons anyway—three, just three, they'd demanded. He stood among his groomsmen, her blockade of bridesmaids barring his way to her until he could pass their challenges, everybody laughing, having a grand time. Out of the corner of his eye, he could see a trickle of red snaking down an exposed drain running along the periphery of her parents' house. Blood from the freshly slaughtered chickens that would become part of the banquet, provided he could indeed successfully explain, in verbalized words, why he wanted to marry her.

Be brave, he exhorted himself, puffing his chest out. So silly now, to think that was how courage manifested for someone like him, a small-town transplant from another small town.

A shiver brought him back to the foot of Maxwell Hill. Light fog foreigned the familiar sight, wrapping his beloved hill like bandages. He walked in through the open halves of the rusty gates, hunching a little against the wind.

Not a mile in and he could already hear the monkeys overhead. He looked up to see a mother with an infant strapped to her chest swaying on the thick electricity cables. How useful those cables were to the families of monkeys. It was almost as if the cables had been installed to provide overhead catwalks and simian flyovers, so that the monkeys never had to share the road with humans. How some of them lorded this over the humans! Those who cowered underneath the monkeys' bald butts, fearing droppings.

He took his favorite shortcut, which branched off the main paved road near a wheezing rivulet that struggled to cast itself down a pile of rocks. Then he was in the jungle proper, and it was like a door had closed behind him. Suddenly the sky darkened and birds cried out louder. Underfoot crunched twigs, pebbles, and insects—mostly ants of a reddish-bronze cast that gave them a man-made sheen in this jungle setting. He saw those ants every day he came up this hill, even when his calf was bothering him and he stuck to the main road, paved and easy, meant for jeeps carrying tourists who wanted views at the top without the climb. He saw the ants scurrying even in the rain, when the shortcut's barely visible dirt path became slippery, and he hiked up as if suspended in space, arms slightly spread, about to topple backward.

In contrast to the ever-present ants, the leeches had appeared only twice since he'd started coming to this hill, which is to say since his wife had left him. Even then, the leeches never showed themselves, instead making their presence known after the fact with the lurid marks they left. He had not known they'd gotten him until he reached the second pavilion, where some of his fellow hikers rested.

"Hey, you're bleeding," the former construction worker said, mopping his face with the shirt he'd just taken off. The second pavilion, situated halfway up the hill, was his handiwork. He'd collected money from Maxwell Hill frequenters like the retired assistant branch manager, and when he'd gotten enough for the wood, cement, and roof tiles, he'd labored until the pavilion had taken root and sprung up between jungle and paved road.

The retired assistant branch manager looked down at his bloodstained socks. A violent fear spasmed in him for just a moment, then vanished. There was no pain. The culprit was long gone.

Later, washing blood off his ankles under a tap fed by spring water, he thought that he would like his death to go the same way—painless, with a retroactive realization. How peaceful it would be, to go about his daily rituals as always, walking, hiking, eating, not thinking about his wife, when suddenly an angel would flap its wings and say to him, "Hey, you're dead." And he would look down and try in vain to find the tiny wounds.

Since then, he'd been on the lookout for leeches every time he hiked. And every time he crossed paths with the retired construction worker, sweaty in the pavilion or running errands on the streets of Taiping, he would ask, "Did the leeches get you this time?" After which he would regurgitate his story of once spotting a wild boar, snorting and in heat, deep in the jungle near a seldom-used shortcut.

How funny people were, always fearing—and yet yearning for—the elusive and harmful. Ceaselessly talking about them, and never about the daily appearances of ants and leaves. Since the retired assistant branch manager had developed eye floaters, he'd seen the leeches maybe half a dozen times before realizing that they were just spots in his eyes. And what did that say about him?

Today he was alone on the shortcut. Most people, even if they wanted to earn their views, trudged up the main paved road and called it "hiking." He did the real thing and tried to go as fast as he could. The last time his daughter had visited him, she'd asked him to show her what he did every day. He'd intuited that she wanted to see how he spent his time, in order to tell how sad or healed he was. That, in turn, would allow her to calibrate her guilt and, potentially, her frequency of visits.

So he chose his favorite shortcut, wanting to impress her. In his excitement, he forgot her body-image issues, and how mercilessly she'd been taunted in sports periods all through primary and secondary school. It was a beautiful day. Tree canopies filtered away the heat of the sun, random rays of light lending the soil a mottled, magical feel, shimmering the whole earth when tree branches jostled with wind. The shortcut weaved through the jungle and passed by a waterfall—really just a mild, short stack of clumsy, tumbling water, but he liked to call it a waterfall anyway. He was eager for his daughter to round a bend and come up against the surprise of the water. He hadn't known he was walking too fast until he turned around to point out the waterfall to her and she wasn't there.

When he backtracked and found her, she was wheezing, sitting hunched over on a fallen trunk. What should he say? He didn't want to embarrass her.

He thought for much longer than he'd have liked, staring down on her crown. At last, he said, "It's a nice day for hiking."

"You're . . . so fast."

"It's only because I do this every day." He was the embarrassed one, after all. "If you came every day, you'd be faster."

"Huh. That's true. I drink beer every day, and I get better and better at it."

He chuckled, then fell into one of his usual silences after someone else's witty remark. Long ago, he'd given up on trying to devise equally witty comebacks or follow-ups. He'd labeled himself a simple man, and that had been that.

"I don't think I can go on anymore."

"There's a waterfall right up there. Just a few steps away."

"A waterfall? Really?"

"Well . . . a small one."

She looked up at him with what he understood as pity. Then, mercifully, she got up and followed him—exaggerating her stumbling, it was true, but also exaggerating her wonderment when the admittedly modest waterfall trickled downward in front of them, her eyes fixed on the hike's reward, as if she were enchanted by its beauty, as if she were lost in meditation of nature's art.

He paused for a break, leaning one palm against a nearby tree. He remembered that he was supposed to be coming up with reasons he loved Taiping.

Well, for one, this was where his daughter had been born and raised. For almost a decade, he'd taken her every year to midautumn festivals at the lake garden, guiding her hands on the surface of dark waters as they launched paper boats with mini candles in place of masts. They never made wishes or anything like that. It was just tradition, something that people did on a specific night each year. Overhead, the full moon shone so bright it almost pulsed, as if fed by the feeble man-made candlelight floating upon the lake.

"Having fun?" he would ask.

His young child would laugh and say, "Yes, yes, so much fun!"

His daughter had not been back to hike with him since he'd unwittingly left her behind. He wondered if he would ever walk through these trees with her again. Squatting by the waterfall, he scooped up a palmful of water. It quickly fled from all sides, back to its whole. But still, his hand was wet.

He straightened up slowly, ready to go on, preparing himself for the usual small talk waiting at the second pavilion. Also waiting would be tea brewed from spring water, and the occasional clementines, clustered together in pyramid form atop the rickety wooden table that the retired carpenter had desultorily assembled.

His feet moved. Dead leaves and dry earth crunched. His eye floaters danced, then snagged on a spot of color. He blinked hard, at first thinking the floaters were getting worse. Then he saw that it was a dirt-hued mushroom with a maroon tinge along the rim of its bulgy cap, worn lopsided, one rakish edge almost touching ground. It was alone.

He had seen it before. Not always in this spot, and not always alone. It, too, walked the jungle as he did. Every time he'd previously seen it, he'd instinctively moved away. Everybody knew mushrooms could be dangerous, especially reddish-brown ones like these. People still talked about that child, unwatched for just a second, dying with dirt under his nails.

Then he felt it on his skin, sudden like standing too close to a sizzling hot wok. Remembered. Smelled it as if he were in a room full of boys soldering, tin fuming. He felt it: what it was like to be young and angry, believing in a fate that was personally interested in him.

His wife had left him, damn it! And maybe old men weren't supposed to feel sorry for themselves, but he didn't feel old, and even if he used his senior discount at the movies it didn't mean he was definitely going to fall asleep, just that sometimes the noise and the drama dulled his mind, which still struggled in tangles over the fact that he really felt he had done absolutely nothing wrong, and yet here he was, and here she wasn't.

He knelt down by the mushroom the way he'd knelt down by the waterfall. Then, knocked over by an unknown impulse, he sat heavily down, nearly squashing the fungus. Myths and legends he'd heard in his boyhood came to him: Young street urchins bestowed with great reservoirs of chi and latent kung fu greatness after ingesting gold mushrooms out of desperate hunger. Medicinal herbs that cured all diseases. A flower that bloomed once a year on a full-moon night, granting immortality to those brave enough to scale the cliffs from which its petals beckoned.

The mushroom felt doughy in his hands. Its stem felt supple, but its cap, with its slender gills, was fragility. From its base, it bled dirt onto his hands. He started brushing it clean, but stopped himself and laughed. Before he'd finished laughing, the mushroom was in his open mouth, and he chewed it once, twice, then swallowed it before he was ready.

There he sat, and there he waited, to see if anything could truly happen to anyone.

DUTY

Ibrahim caught himself shaking his head at an empty room. In disgust, he threw down the newspaper he had spread at face level, annoyed that the lousy state of the country could manipulate him so physically, like a puppet. And now his fingers were smeared with black, the nonsense he read actually marking him. Sighing angrily, he got up to wash his hands, not noticing that his head was set to shaking again.

Malaysia was going to the dogs. They were *releasing* that idiot woman who had pretended to write those disgusting poems. Just a young person who'd blundered, they said. No, no hate in what she'd done, not at all, not at all! Tch. More than anything, he resented the rabble-rousers for muddying his thoughts. There was no benefit to embroiling his mind and soul—which he strove so hard to keep turned toward holiness—in the childish filth put out by headline chasers. His hands and brains were put to much better use behind the scenes, as it were, where no limelight shone and yet there was so much good done. For example, the work he did with the state Religious Department. It wasn't just talking, talking, talking, which anybody could do. This was grassroots and on-the-ground, tackling concrete issues one human soul at a time. *He* was a real patriot.

True, the RD was no police force, nor was it as far-reaching as a rival volunteer corps whose successes included sting operations that sniffed out buildings full of illegal immigrants, capturing them for deportation all in one fell swoop. Ibrahim's work had a more personal touch to it. It wasn't just rounding up foreign parasites clearly on the wrong side of the law. In his work, the focus was instead on cultivating and nurturing the young, strayed sons and daughters of Malaysia. These were often mere kids he dealt with, after all, barely mature enough to think beyond immediate gratification. Ibrahim was given the chance to be a father figure for these wayward youngsters who had but momentarily deviated from their true paths.

What he did required much more finesse. He was handling issues that were maybe more gray than strictly black and white. Black and white was leaving your own country in a little fishing boat by cover of night, and then plundering innocent, upright citizens when you found out jobs did not, in fact, grow on Malaysian trees. Gray was the teenage girl from last week, barely older than his own daughter.

Ibrahim scratched his chin, seeking the abrasive texture of his short beard. His wife peeked around the doorframe, her features drooping into worry when she saw that her husband was staring fixedly, eyes glazed, at his own reflection in the bathroom mirror.

"Dinner time." The bath tiles echoed her voice.

Ibrahim cleared his throat and said he would be there soon.

It must have scared his wife, too, his nightmares that had begun visiting every evening. That sweet woman. After patiently enduring the first few nights of his sweaty, flailing limbs, she'd started making him herbal tea before bed. But it caused Ibrahim to struggle up for bathroom runs in the middle of the night, grunting, and the nightmares then actually multiplied, since every travel from wakefulness to sleep was a brand-new trigger for another version of the same nightmare.

Next, she'd suggested Western classical music. He'd tried it for ten minutes. It only bewildered him. Flutes and violas and trombones, things from another realm—it was all so alien, and it made him uneasy with its strangeness.

In the end, he'd given up on sleep and signed on for nocturnal operations with the town's RD. They lived in a sleepy, traditional town, nothing like the big-city lights of Kuala Lumpur or Penang, but in small towns too there were bad influences and crooked elements at play. If God kept him up and wished him to have more waking hours than most men, then he would not squander the extra time granted to him.

"Bang!" his wife called from the dining room.

"Ya!" he shouted back, leaving the bathroom at last.

His wife and daughter sat waiting at the dining table, plates and bowls of food between them. Out of the corner of his eye, he gleaned his wife's glance of worry.

Retirement threw him off, she was probably thinking. He'll adjust to it, she might hope. Give him time. It's only been a month. God will guide.

That was his wife, Marina—hopefully patient, if nothing else.

He scooped up a piece of beef and cradled it with his fingers. Across the table, his daughter was chewing contentedly, right hand loose, ready for the next scoop of food.

Last week a teenage girl, barely older than his own Siti, had peered with disbelief from the amoral dark car in which she had been trapped, trying to see around the flashlight beams and make out the faces of the men who shone them. It'd been a hot night. She and her partner in crime had cranked down all the car windows.

Whose cage of sin was this scratched blue Proton Saga? Ibrahim, putting off the mental processing of such an unbelievable thing as a young Malay girl willingly entwining with a Chinese boy, started pondering the ownership of the vehicle.

It must be his, this hairless young man, engorged pupils blinking in the light of justice that cleared away the dangerous darkness of a tree's canopy, their intended shelter from discovery.

Now the boy was putting on a brave face as Ibrahim's RD brothers practiced the highly effective tactic of divide and conquer, ordering the boy to step out of his car. Stay inside, they gestured to the girl, palms pushing against the night air.

When the boy emerged, he had all of his clothing on without disarray. Ibrahim breathed out heavily. Perhaps they had arrived in time to preserve her purity after all.

In the back seat the girl shrank, hunched in belated modesty. One of his colleagues leaned close and hissed, jeering, "Is Chinese penis really that good?"

Ibrahim felt exceptional sorrow then. To think, how unfair it was. The boy, the mentally stronger of the two (*sometimes* the mentally stronger, he heard his wife's voice correcting him gently), instigates the whole disgraceful mess, tempts the poor girl to give up her natural honor and sense of shame to commit khalwat. And yet he gets to walk away free, without a mar on his life, because he is not Muslim and thus not subject to the jurisdiction of the RD or the Syariah courts. The best they could do was shine strong battery-powered light into his eyes, shake him up a bit. But the poor girl, so young, has sinned! Has sinned and will forever be under the scrutiny and judgment of both men and God. Ibrahim sighed once more. The silver lining was that she, at least, fell under their jurisdiction. He would do what he could for her.

That night there was no scheduled RD operation, and so Ibrahim had no choice but to put himself into a horizontal position under a blanket and close his eyes, first gently, then tightly, listening to his wife's breathing, waiting for it to slow and lengthen.

She had massaged his shoulders right before bed and he had allowed it, willing himself to unclench, understanding that she was just trying to help.

Tonight, the nightmare started out as an audio-only presentation: a loud clacking of what sounded like high heels on tar. Gradually, his dream-eyes adjusted to the black blank, and he saw that, once again, it was night in a marsh.

AUDIO   VISUAL

AUDIO	VISUAL
Loud clacking on tar.	Night.
MADU: "Spread out! Don't follow me!"	One hand holding up bunches of a purple dress, running feet in heels, tar road.
Loud clacking abruptly turns into subdued squishing sounds of heels sinking into grass and soil.	Running heels abruptly sidestepping from tar road onto the beginnings of a riverbank.

AUDIO	VISUAL
Rustling of grass, panting.	Heels coming off of stumbling feet.
Rustling of fabric, different panting.	Cut to entryway of a nondescript building, where volunteers, all men, herd a group of sequined evening dresses from within the well-lit foyer into the gloom of evening.
Rustling of grass, different panting.	Cut to a different pair of heels coming off a different pair of running feet.
Rustling of fabric, different panting.	Cut to an evening gown being forcibly torn off a shoulder.
Rustling of grass, different panting.	Cut to bare feet scissoring.
Rustling of fabric, different panting.	Cut to previous evening gown being completely torn off, revealing a torso.
Rustling of grass, different panting.	Cut to a river lit up by moonlight.

AUDIO	VISUAL
Rustling of fabric, different panting.	Cut to discarded heels, suddenly obscured by an evening gown dropped from above. Pan up to bare legs and buttocks.
Rustling of grass, different panting.	Pan out over moonlit river.
Sound of spitting.	Cut to volunteer spitting on the ground in disgust.
Sound of splashing.	Cut to a shadow leaping off the bank into the river.
Sound of spitting.	Cut to volunteer being spat at in the face.
Sound of splashing.	Cut to two more shadows throwing themselves into the river.
VOLUNTEER: "Spread out! Find the ones who escaped!"	Cut to Volunteer A picking up a stout branch from the ground.
MADU: "Spread out! Or they'll find us!"	Cut to Madu swimming backward while gesturing wildly for Mawar and Omar to keep their distance.

AUDIO	VISUAL
In the distance, the call for Azan prayers transmitting through the air from the nearest masjid.	Cut to Omar in his room, praying on his prayer mat.
Shears snipping.	Cut to Volunteer A going into his garden.
Brush pulling through hair.	Cut to Omar brushing a wig in his room.
Shears snipping.	Cut to Volunteer A pruning a tree.
Brush pulling through hair.	Cut to young Omar, grinning wickedly, cutting the hair off a doll while his sister bawls beside him.
	Cut to a wig floating on moonlit water.
Sounds of splashing and spitting intermingled.	Cut to Omar and Mawar climbing out of the river onto the bank, Omar almost naked, Mawar's waterlogged evening dress dragging.

AUDIO	VISUAL
OMAR: "Madu! Mana Madu?"	Omar's face, distressed.
MAWAR: "She swam away from us."	The back of Mawar's head, long wet hair.
	Cut to a brightly hued wig floating on sunlit water.
Rustling of fabric and grass.	Cut to one hand holding up bunches of a purple dress. Pan out to reveal child of indeterminate sex discover- ing purple dress and drag- ging it through the grass.
	Blue skies.
Rustling of fabric, panting. "Sayang, oh, sayang!"	Cut to Omar kissing and undressing his wife in a sunlit room.
NEWSCASTER: "A transexual beauty pag- eant being held at a resort near here was broken up by the Kelantan Islamic Reli- gious Affairs Department. Its chief assistant director Abdul Aziz Mohd Nor said	Cut to cutting of hair. Pan out to reveal Omar's wife trimming her ends in front of the television. Omar's wife's hair drops in clumps onto newspaper spread out on the floor. Pan

AUDIO   VISUAL

AUDIO	VISUAL
the group, in their twenties and thirties, was detained at about 10:00 p.m. on Friday while posing in women's dresses. Three of them managed to get away by diving into a nearby river . . ."	in to reveal a news article beginning with "A transexual beauty pageant being held at a resort near here was broken up . . ."
Shears snipping, faint.	Falling strands hit a small mound of collected hair on the newspaper.
OMAR'S WIFE: "Abang, where are you going?"	Cut to a brightly hued wig floating on sunlit water.
Shears snipping, loud.	Cut to Omar bursting out of his front door. Pan to reveal his neighbor, Volunteer A, pruning branches in his garden.
Rustle of grass, panting.	Cut to Omar running through grass.
Rustle of fabric, panting.	Omar taking off his shirt, his bare torso.

AUDIO   VISUAL

Sound of spitting.   Omar jumping into the
                      river, one hand still holding
                      on to his shirt.

Sound of splashing.   Omar swimming against
                       the current, spitting out
                       mouthfuls of water as he
                       advances.

Sound of spitting.   Omar climbing half out
                      of the water onto the bank,
                      where Madu's naked upper
                      body lies sprawled.

Sound of splashing.   Close-up of Omar's face,
                       tears, snot, mouthing inau-
                       dible words.

Shears snipping in a   Cut to Omar's wife at
regular beat, each snip   the window, watching
a second apart, as in   a pruned branch falling
a clock ticking.   through the air.

Snip.   Omar no longer crying,
         wiping thick makeup off
         Madu's face with his soaked
         shirt.

Snip.   Omar, turning Madu's face
         to the left,

AUDIO   VISUAL

Snip.	to the right,
Snip.	wiping off one last smudge of eyeliner.
Snip.	One hand holding the dirty shirt, bunched up,
Snip.	plunging into the river,
Snip.	another hand joining the first in the water
Snip.	to scrub the dirty shirt back
Snip.	and forth
Snip.	against itself.
Snip.	Shirt, raised out of the water,
Snip.	dripping,
Snip.	twisted to let water
Snip.	out.
Snip.	Hands struggling

AUDIO   VISUAL

Snip.   to put the shirt

Snip.   on Madu's body.

Snip.   Cut to a brightly hued wig
        floating on sunlit water.

Snip.   Pan out to reveal Omar

Snip.   holding a stout branch

Snip.   reaching out to draw the
        wig in toward shore.

Snip.   Cut to Omar on the shore,
        dripping wet,

Snip.   digging a hole near the
        roots of a tree,

Snip.   the wet wig lying beside the
        gradually enlarged hole.

Snip.   Cut to sunlit water, ripples
        forming where the wig
        used to float.

Snip.   A hip-

Snip.   po-

AUDIO   VISUAL

Snip.   po-

Snip.   ta-

Snip.   mus

Snip.   rising out of the

Snip.   water.

Snip.

Snip.

Snip.

Snip.

Snip.

Snip.

Snip.

Snip.

Snip.

Snip.

Next to him, close to Ibrahim's face, the whites of his wife's eyes shone dully in the dark. He felt her hand reaching for his.

"You were calling his name," she said.

He tried to think of something to say.

"It's been so many years," she said. "You are not responsible for him, even if he is your brother. He made his own choices. He was old enough to think for himself."

For his virgin raid, Ibrahim had gone to Jaya supermarket and bought a pair of Bata shoes. That had been a week ago. The shoes waited for him now, still shiny and alien next to his worn rubber slippers. The sales clerk had said that the shoes were best for badminton.

He let himself fall back for that very first operation, bringing up the rear of the RD raid party. The moon was out that night, pockmarked and almost full.

One of his RD brothers turned to reassure him that this was one of their "regular" raids, and that they did not expect any extraordinary developments. Ibrahim wanted to ask what the other man meant, but he was facing ahead again, and his back was ruler straight. This one had a goatee, which therefore meant his name was . . . Safee. Safee's hand swept a flashlight in steady arcs at waist level, as if showcasing selected scenery—to their left a padang, clumps of wild lalang reaching for each other's shadows with every gust of wind; to their right a silhouette of a tree growing next to what looked like tatters of a soccer goal. Ibrahim and his new RD brothers walked on the paved road running alongside the padang. Ahead, someone's slippers slapped loudly with each step. Ibrahim was glad for his new shoes, quiet and solid in a rubbery way.

For the past half mile or so, the paved road had curved past residential houses, normal-looking ones with dim lights leaking through curtains and potted plants strewn about front yards. Then the normal houses thinned, and they were advancing past a giant block of oddly shaped blackness, as if someone had tried to scale up Lego pieces. An old tire factory, Safee informed Ibrahim.

Against his bidding, a dream-like scene visited: men wearing nothing but tires around their waists, covering their privates, trying to push-roll other men wearing nothing but tires lying on their sides. That was what lay within the misshapen Lego block, he was convinced. High up, a man wearing a dress swayed limply from the ceiling beams, seated in a tire swing, legs kicking ineffectually to propel himself. Ibrahim's ex-brother was there, too, hanging from his neck off a tire noose, his hands holding up the sides of his calf-length skirt, curtsying midair.

The volunteers ahead slowed, flashlight beams arcing lower and closer to the ground. Ibrahim peered. They were approaching dirt lanes branching off the main paved road. Row houses flanked the lanes, looking just like the terraced houses they had passed not too long ago. Looking, in fact, like row houses all over the state, including the one that was Ibrahim's own two-story, thirty-year-mortgage unit.

Except these units up ahead were unnaturally dark: darker than the road they walked on, and darker even than the trees bowing over the wedges of black roofs. A ghost town? Ibrahim was confused. Right in his backyard, too. What had happened here? A terrible fire that had licked out a whole swathe of land? An entire village killed decades ago by Japanese soldiers, never rehabilitated? How had he not known about—and then he did know, the realization falling upon him as if from a great height.

It had many names: Kampung Mak Nyah, Ah Kua Village, Sodomia. Ibrahim had actually been here once, *inside*, but he had approached it from a different road, not from this narrow tar one that slithered past the back of factory buildings. This must be the other end of the No Man's Land. No Man, because all the men here did not want to be men. They wanted to be ugly women, willingly throwing away their lives to settle for that.

Of course he thought about Omar. How could he not? And again he wondered if things would have been different if he had not gone so far away for university. But he'd had no idea, no inkling that such strange desires coiled within his own brother. If Omar had only confided in him, Ibrahim would have done anything at all to anchor him in home and all that was holy. Instead, Ibrahim had gone away to study at the country's best university, and his brother had ridden away for good on his motorcycle, enticed by the wrong kind of desire.

It must have been latent then, when he had come here with Omar. That was back when things were as one expected them to be, and his brother was normal, just a regular skinny kid in secondary school. They were front-to-back on their shared motorcycle, going fast. The wind rippled their T-shirts, tight against chests but swelling out and away from spines, flapping like flags.

It must have been Omar's idea to go gawk at the transvestites. Ibrahim had probably thought it a dare, or an adventure. Like going to the zoo, except this was free and less safe with the absence of bars and moats and therefore more exciting. The attraction was the mak nyahs, said to pose in various stages of undress in the dark yards of the dark houses, waiting for customers.

In a flash, Ibrahim wondered if it had been his fault after

all, for agreeing to go along when Omar was still so young and so impressionable. What if that had been the catalyst? Had it all begun that night, when they rounded the corner and the motorcycle's headlights picked out a seated body?

An arm threw itself over the spotlighted face, but the mak nyah's body remained pivoted toward them. Ibrahim's eyes sought the presence of breasts. But it was too dark to gauge their authenticity under that baby doll top, headlights only intensifying shadows and rounding contours. The brothers breathed in silence. Ibrahim tried to think of something witty to say.

Then the mak nyah made to stand up, the motion triggering a rustling. The grass grew as tall as her knees, Ibrahim finally noticed. Behind him, he felt Omar's chest stiffen. A protective instinct rose in Ibrahim. His right hand tightened around the handlebars. Out of the corner of his eye, something metallic glinted. He jerked up to see a row of bras hanging on a rattan clothesline strung through tree branches, swaying in the breeze but somehow seeming dense and heavy.

His brother screamed in his ear. By the time he refocused his sight on the transvestite, mismatching knuckles and cleavage were already right up against his face. Ibrahim understood that the free show was over, and that it was time to pay.

He whipped his head around his shoulder to gostan out of the dark street, catching one last glimpse of what they had come to see before they sped away. She was grinning triumphantly, mouth open wide and immobile.

Not once did he check the rearview mirror to see what expression his brother's face formed.

So much older he was now, an age far along enough to command respect from most, but not yet so over the hill as to invite suspicions of weakness. He felt the perfection of his fit with the RD, savoring it as he kept pace with the other volunteers.

That first night, they did not find anything or anybody. "The mak nyahs must have had a tipster," Safee said while shaking his head, disappointed that they could not show Ibrahim what it was all about.

The next night was more rewarding, even though it was a small catch of only three transvestites. As they wrapped up, Ibrahim resolved to steel his heart against what the work required. They had chased the mak nyahs into the fields and caught the ones cornered in a cul-de-sac. Those were shoved and shouted at to subdue their wailing, and one had unfortunately fallen on the ground and refused to get up, so a few of them had had to drag her a bit. Another's purse was roughly yanked from her clutch and rifled through.

But it was for a purpose. The end result was extracted confessions and vows of repentance. One of the mak nyahs, the one who had tripped and fallen, cried messily in an absurd, hoarse voice. Ibrahim felt so sorry for her he stuffed five ringgit into the reformed captive's manicured hands, then immediately regretted doing it, of course, for what would it look like? Like a filthy transaction, that's what.

He looked around to see if anyone had noticed. All around him were men, busying themselves in semidarkness, everyone finding something to do, even though they far outnumbered the mak nyahs.

That night, he felt his way across his bedroom and slipped in next to his wife. He was too rattled to sleep. Looking at his wife's curly hair next to him, Ibrahim felt waves of guilt. He had compromised the purity of their marriage by a thoughtless act of kindness.

At that moment, Ibrahim vowed to be an even better man than he already was. He would make up for the roughness some of his fellow RD volunteers exhibited by being a thoughtful, avuncular counterpart. He would be the one who delivered sermons harsh on the surface, but with a tender-hearted core. When the perpetrators were sufficiently shame-faced, he would soften his tone and remind them how much of their precious futures were at stake, and look! In their sweaty hands, this shrinking window to save it all.

Yes, next time he would play this role, and he would play it perfectly. Let no one say the RD was just a bunch of wannabe vigilantes on power trips. His mission was to save souls. It would be known.

The next night, Ibrahim had a different nightmare.

He was on a raid of a hotel, the sordid one at the edge of town. In the lobby, scruffy carpets raised clouds of dirt ash at their extremities, in corners no one tread. Naked light bulbs concentrated cones of light on the front desk and lit up, weakly, the door yawning into a dark stairway.

In the background, atmospheric sounds of pipes shuddering, cockroaches clicking, and far-off trucks stumbling swirled in a bad blend. The hotel smelled of youth, which is to say unsanitary in a nevertheless glorious way. Dream-Ibrahim and his dream-brothers crept silently up the dim stairs. They were purposeful.

At the door they sought, the man in the lead produced keys and noiselessly inserted them into the keyhole. The door swung, and dream-Ibrahim saw a tiny room that was all bed and floor-length curtains. On the bed were two misguided, young teenagers.

Oh, expanse of skin! Cream and sea fronds! Saxophones

and bassoons! The girl gasped silently and turned around to look straight at her father, dream-Ibrahim.

"Your hair is not long enough!" he roared at her.

Ibrahim jolted awake, shaking. *How dare you?* he seethed, breathing hard. *Give me such dreams. Dream such things. How dare you?* He was furious at something he could not name.

"Bang, be careful tonight," his wife said at dinner, eyes lowered to her food.

"Tonight? Where are you going?" Siti asked. Ibrahim shuddered. Her face was an unblemished patch of sweetness. So young. His eyes involuntarily lowered to seek out her bosom, wanting to gauge any changes, but the tabletop reached just north of her breastbone; she was so short still. Her hair fell straight until it met the obstacles that were her round shoulders, and there it started to curl charmingly, in obedient waves, uniform like the whorls of the smooth wooden posts at the end of their staircase.

When he left for the RD, the outside air was so humid it felt like walking through Tiger Balm. The patch between Ibrahim's neck and shoulder blades ached, and he felt himself slouching. He thought that he must be tired.

The walk to the RD headquarters was short. As he hurried along, he renewed his promise. Tonight, he would calmly help whoever it was they caught, especially the girls and women. If any of his brothers made threats or exhibited roughness in general, he would step in and tilt the balance. He straightened, feeling stronger with purpose.

All along the way, Ibrahim fingered the switch of the flashlight in his hand. Fleeting, distorted circles of light clicked audibly on and off, picking out loose gravel, pebbles, and tough little tufts of weeds that sprang up through cracks in the tar. The flashlight felt right in his clutch, as if custom-made for him.

Around him, families slept, bickered, watched mediocre state TV or satellite programming. A few figures sat outdoors, letting the night breeze evaporate their sweat. Smokers. Old people. Dirty dogs.

When he passed under a streetlamp, his flashlight's click ceased to produce the orb of light he was used to. He paused and looked up at the bigger, stronger light source that swallowed whole the output of his torch. Squinting, he could make out swarms of moths and miscellaneous insects batting themselves about haphazardly. He turned his flashlight on one more time, just to see it fail to do anything, subsumed.

By the time he reached the RD building, his collared cotton shirt was gently sticking to the small of his back. The building was grand by most local standards, the exterior a series of lofty columns topped off with faux-gold dome arches.

Inside, his colleagues lounged, drinking strong tea, adjusting brimmed caps, testing flashlights. A short discussion took place, and it was agreed they would take Safee and Yaacob's cars tonight, since those were roomier. It looked set to be another regular night of aimless patrolling, which Ibrahim quite enjoyed. It meant hours of strolling the main and back streets of this town he loved so much, feeling his contributions to its safety and moral cleanliness while everyone else slumbered, trusting and oblivious. As the night deepened, the air would cool, and that, too, was delightful.

But then the mobile phone of Aziz, their leader, rang. He turned his back on the other men and issued mutterings of "Ya" and "Ah ah" to the west wall of the room. When he hung up and turned around, his eyes were glistering.

"Change of plans," he barked. They would be raiding Hotel Fajar tonight, that seedy place on top of the town's second-biggest supermarket. The phone call was a tip-off from the front-desk clerk who had checked in a young Malay couple just a few minutes ago. He had watched the couple ascend to their room, leaning into each other unsteadily.

The room perked and buzzed. Ibrahim blinked. For a second, he thought someone had put a color filter over the lights, maybe yellow or orange; the rays illuminating the space were warmer, and yet shriller at the same time. He stood up. He understood—or perhaps it was the room's mood he picked up—that something big would happen tonight.

"How much did that loser ask for?" someone asked Aziz.

Aziz muttered grouchily in a low voice. Ibrahim stooped to retie the laces on his Bata shoes. He did not hear what was said.

Now they were in Yaacob's van, a black box charging down streets toward its target. Rocking in the car against Aziz's warm thigh, Ibrahim absentmindedly looked down at his lap. He started. His right hand was clenched tightly around his flashlight. Squinting his eyes, he looked out of their corners at the other men's hands. They were empty, open and relaxed. It was an indoor expedition, after all. The suspects had nowhere to run, unless they tried the window ledges, which some of the male offenders did from time to time, Ibrahim was told. But they never got far, and it was always just awkward for them, perched or dangling.

When the boxy car came to a shuddering stop and the engine was killed, Ibrahim became abruptly aware of his heart, as unrelenting as cicadas in the bushes. The car seat made a loud, rude noise when he slid off to touch gravelly ground.

Ibrahim stood still in the balmy night. Craning his neck, he saw that only a couple of windows were lit, veiled by curtains. The hotel's sign was small and off white in a dirty way. Near its entrance were bags and cardboard boxes overflowing with rubbish, refuse from the supermarket, obviously picked over by tramps, mongrels, whomever.

Inside, the clerk gestured excitedly. He was thin and his shoulders hunched forward, bearing a head with untidy hair but an immaculate little mustache. Ibrahim looked at him with contempt. Even though they were supposed to be on the same side, helping the town, Ibrahim did not feel a man who took money in exchange for information was trustworthy. If he truly cared about the welfare of the wayward young souls upstairs, Ibrahim thought, the clerk could have simply refused to give them a room, could he have not? "No vacancy"—easy enough.

The clerk was slumped over his desk, shaking his head to Aziz and miming sorrow. Ibrahim turned away. There was no functional furniture to be seen in the lobby. He started counting his fellow volunteers, milling about with nowhere to sit. Before he could finish, he saw Aziz sweeping the room with his gaze, trying to catch everyone's eyes. It was time.

The door yawning into the dark stairway was propped open by a rubber wedge shaped like a miniature slice of Western cake.

Up the stairs they went, some trying not to breathe hard. Ibrahim clutched his belt buckle and yanked upward while jerking it from side to side. His other hand touched the banister. Dusty.

When the men ahead of him slowed, Ibrahim suddenly realized the disadvantages of bringing up the rear. He would be the last to see the sinners, censored here and there by the arms, shoulders, and necks of his colleagues. No, he must—he pushed his way past a couple men and groped for the top of the stairs. But the door was already opening.

There was a shriek. The girl, eyes half-closed, saw the religious men before the boy did. Ibrahim made out that she was struggling to escape from the enclosure created by the boy's body, his arms planked straight into the thin mattress, when a second ago she must have welcomed the screen of his flesh slotted between her and heaven, God's eye shining.

Ibrahim shut his eyes tightly. From behind came an impatient shove. The others were rushing into the room, while he remained standing, holding on to the doorframe.

It wasn't his daughter. Of course it wasn't. Hadn't he just seen her at dinner, picking out limp onion strands and beaching them on the edge of her plate? Wasn't she a safe, dark lump in her room when he'd looked in on her, flashlight in hand?

Where *was* his flashlight? For a spinning second, Ibrahim felt very lost. He wondered whether it was true that he had a daughter. How had she appeared in his life?

And then the girl on the motel mattress sat up, insisting that she was a married woman, pushing at her husband to go get their laminated marriage card to show the volunteers. She was about to cry. Ibrahim opened his eyes. He thought about his wife, Marina, about Siti, about Omar. He took a deep breath and tried to feel good and strong. He was here to help, after all. Wasn't he?

SO SHE GETS HOME

Isa blinked her eyes shut in the strong sunlight. Her eyes were watery, stinging. It was impossible, and yet it seemed as if the sun shone fiercer in freedom. The detention center's courtyard was just a few steps behind her, beyond that tall metal gate boiling to the touch. Was the sun really weaker in there? Maybe the guard towers blocked light. She turned around to peer into her prison of eight months and met, instead, the eyes of a uniformed man adjusting a machine gun on his shoulder.

Here came her mother. Isa could see the disapproving tongue ready for deployment, glinting well-oiled in its trench. There was also something else in her mother's eyes, something she had never seen before, an emotion seeming to shrivel her mother's eyes inward into their clamshells. Was it pity? Isa knew she looked terrible, especially so since her hunger strike. She could not see well. The sun was too bright.

She stood, immobile and yet unstable, like a pebble waiting to be kicked. There was a car with tinted windows parked across the street. She tried to peer through the windows. What it must feel like to drive a car. Such power, to bring your abode along with you, as safe as a hermit crab.

Here reached her mother, already throwing out arms to draw her in. For some reason Isa thought of fish swimming into wide-open traps. "I'm sorry!" she cried like a coward.

"I didn't say anything," her mother said, stroking Isa's hair, except it was terribly tangled and it seemed like a punishment, after all, as Isa knew it would be, when her mother jerked her fingers free.

"You've lost so much weight . . . You're like a bird, all bones."

Isa sniffled, saying nothing. Her body was doing all the talking now.

At home, her mother spread a mini banquet in front of Isa. A jolly red cloth had been thrown over the rickety dining table. The centerpiece was a whole chicken, freshly killed that very afternoon. Its head curved back upon its neck, eyes slits, beak very slightly parted. The beginnings of a comb sprouted along the ridge of its crown, a tumorous mohawk.

This was a day of celebration.

The kitchen was the same, yellow square tiles on the floor and one corner of a ceiling panel loose, there, near where the geckos loved to hang out, a triangular yawn hinting at darkness and decay.

"Did you know that American girl who pretended to be you and wrote those . . . poems?"

Isa's mother meant well. She had absolutely planned on holding her tongue until after poor Isabella had had time to enjoy a good meal, digest, and relax. But Isa was already glumming, eyelids heavy as lace curtains on a hot afternoon. Furrows deepened on her face, grimacing, and it was plain she *would* be unhappy the whole night.

"She didn't pretend to be me. She didn't even know I existed," Isa replied.

"How do you know!"

"I read the newspaper." Blank stare at her blank dinner plate.

"If she hadn't come forward . . . you would still be rotting in there! Stupid girl . . ." Isa's mother stabbed her chopsticks eastward. "Why, Isabella? Why did you want everyone to think you wrote those poems? Don't you know how worried I've been? I lost weight, my blood pressure went up, the doctors say I've taken ten years off my life . . ."

Isa's body spoke up again and answered, an upturned waiter's hand swiveling outward with grace, arm pivoting swift and smooth on the sharp point of an elbow. *I was nothing. What I did, my sacrifice, mattered only when I had a national stage, a stage conjured up by those who supported my selflessness. A stage given fleshly weight by those, even more numerous, who hated the poems' shocking outspokenness.*

Now that I have been restored to a no one, it does not count, none of it. I cannot claim the defiant act, but it also cannot be held against me because I am, once more, nothing.

Her mother shook her head, eyes downcast, tears swilling about, marinating sockets.

Isa scraped a hand forward along the dinner table, as if making to sneak off food from her mother's plate. The hand touched nothing. Isa parted her lips and whispered, "Mama. Don't cry. I'm home."

It had the effect she wanted, but she felt indescribably foolish. Since she had been released, every phrase out of her mouth rang hollow as a rice hull to her.

She lingered as long as she could, resorting even to eating rice grain by grain. When her mother tired of watching her eat, she stood up, hand pressing down on the tabletop for leverage. A few minutes later, she came back with a newspaper clipping, clutched almost shyly to her stomach. Isa looked at the reverse side of what her mother had yet to show her: half a headline made meaningless by being incomplete; a weight-loss ad model with legs lopped off; part of a write-up about two toddlers, siblings, who had been locked away and starved. *There are always two sides to every story*, her brain transmitted.

"What?" Isa asked. "What is that?" She grimaced at the snow bank of rice she had made on one side of her plate, remembering the reporters, thick camera straps lashed with sweat. They'd been waiting outside Kamunting when she walked out from the detention center. Had there been sun-vying flashes aimed at her face, or had she imagined it?

Her mother set the clipping down. Right side up, the paper's boundaries made sense, neatly marking off a single editorial about Isa. No, not about her—about Miss Sodomy the Poet. There she was, a pretty foreign woman smiling down, sunlight exploding her head from behind, obscuring chunks of hair and crown in whiteness. Next to her, Isa looked gaunt in her own picture, the monochrome newspaper shade making it resemble headshots placed at the feet of coffins.

Ah, Isa, she chided herself. Why was the first instinct to compare her looks against the other woman's? They weren't feuding over a man or something. Instead, the winnings had been an identity, a role. And she, the real Isabella, the fake poet, had lost.

She read the clipping too fast and had to start over, forcing herself to register every word. Her eyes kept drifting back to the two photos, slotted side by side. It seemed the columnist could not make up his mind about who was demon and who angel. The foreign woman, real name "Sarah," was praised for speaking out as an ally of Malaysia, but lampooned for using an Asian pseudonym. Isa was given credit for not being an apathetic young woman, having attended protests and even suffered detention for a cause, but it was obviously irresponsible of her to claim authorship for what she had not written. Even the poems were first written off as an immature joke, then lauded for the effect they had brought by pissing off the government so much it had locked Isa away, which had in turn sparked street protests and ultimately raised international awareness of Malaysia's plight. The theme was murky: unintended good was the best kind of good. Writers and other artists could not help but be bad, weak, selfish, and "thinking only of small pictures." But a people—a nation—could appropriate the egoists' flawed creations and transform them into powerful tools.

Sarah had consented to an interview, where Isa had not. Sarah was now artist-in-residence at an elite private kindergarten in New Mexico. In the clipping, she explained that she had chosen the pseudonym "Isa" because the acronym ISA was short for Internal Security Act, the subject of the poem's rage and fire. "What had you hoped to achieve by writing those poems under a pseudonym?" the columnist asked Sarah. The poet replied that art was its own means and ends, an answer the asker particularly scorned. "They are not your poems anymore," he informed her in his column. "They belong to Malaysians now, angry and ready for change, and we will not thank you."

Long after Isa had finished taking in the words of the editorial, she sat there, staring at the piece of paper, believing that she was fooling her mother into thinking she was still reading, not knowing that time was passing much faster for her than for her mother. Eventually, her mother stood up. Isa sighed.

She left her mother, saying she needed a bath. When she reached the bathroom, she pressed a button in the middle of the doorknob. It sank down easily under her thumb. The door was supposedly locked now, but who knew? It didn't have throw latches or slide bolts, those visual affirmations available on the door of her cell.

She averted her eyes from the huge mirror and stripped, tugging fast and rough. Somewhere in the cicadas' kingdom under the moon, a car engine rumbled deep, the dark night's own hunger pangs.

In the bathtub, she stood, hesitating. The hot shower dial was pointed to number three. She had forgotten what that meant. She shivered, a whole-body kind of violent vibration. A gust of night air pushed through the small barred window right next to the showerhead. There was a covering for the window, thick opaque glass that fit over the square like an airtight lid, but tonight, the glass lid was propped wide open. Maybe someone had been wiping down the frames, to prevent rusting.

Isa peered out at the smooth black sky marred by acne stars, wondering if anyone could see her. If anyone was watching. Maybe up there on the waist of the hill, where the mound nipped in as if corseted. Maybe on the top floor of the house two doors down, with binoculars adjusting.

She turned on the shower. A stream shattered itself against her body, fragments scattering off. The window stayed open, funneling in breezes, counteracting water that was too hot. Let them watch. Here she was, shallow scabs and mottled bruises. She was utterly alone, even if they were out there keeping tabs on her. Like a fish launched up higher than it had ever been before, by the tallest wave it had ever seen, then stranded on the beach, no wave strong enough now to go that far again and bring it back home.

Here she was, Isabella Sin, poet and revolutionary. They had given her those titles, and she had accepted them. Now she simply had to become who she was.

ACKNOWLEDGMENTS

A deep bow of respect to Louise Meriwether, who is a great force and an inspiration. I will strive to always tell the truth, as you so bravely do. And a deep bow to Shirley Geok-lin Lim, for inspiring me when I was first fumbling my way to becoming a writer. Much gratitude to:

Jennifer Baumgardner, Melissa R. Sipin, Jamia Wilson and the Feminist Press, and *TAYO Literary Magazine* for creating the Louise Meriwether First Book Prize to support the work of women and nonbinary writers of color. Ana Castillo and Tayari Jones for their generosity and kind words. Lauren Rosemary Hook, Suki Boynton, Jisu Kim, Drew Stevens, Lucia Brown, and everyone at the Feminist Press for giving this book shape, form, and presence.

Kassim Ahmad, Saari Sungib, and all who have written with painful clarity about their detentions under the Internal Security Act. *Universiti Kedua* and *Sengsara Kem Kamunting: Kisah Hidup dalam Penjara ISA* are brave accounts confronting injustice.

Father. Mother. Brother. For cheer and support, no matter where I am (and perhaps despite my life decisions). Teachers and poetry folks from the Northwestern undergraduate writing program, for welcoming with open arms a nonnative English speaker and engineering major to boot. Anna Keesey, Averill Curdy Murr, Brian Bouldrey, Reginald Gibbons, Robyn Schiff, Sheila Donohue. Ellen Cantrell. Jan Clausen. It's been a while, but I remember what I learned from all of you.

And boundless love to David Joseph, for crouching patiently by me when I am temporarily defeated, down in the dust.

The Feminist Press is a nonprofit educational organization founded to amplify feminist voices. FP publishes classic and new writing from around the world, creates cutting-edge programs, and elevates silenced and marginalized voices in order to support personal transformation and social justice for all people.

See our complete list of books at **feministpress.org**

Founded in 2016, **The Louise Meriwether First Book Prize** is awarded to a debut work by a woman or non-binary author of color in celebration of the legacy of Louise Meriwether. Presented by the Feminist Press in partnership with *TAYO Literary Magazine*, the prize seeks to uplift much-needed stories that shift culture and inspire a new generation of writers.